Courage

Hive Honey Quest, Volume 3

Amarah Parks

Published by Amarah Parks LLC, 2024.

This is a work of fiction. Similarities to real people, places, or events are entirely coincidental.

COURAGE

First edition. September 27, 2024.

Copyright © 2024 Amarah Parks.

ISBN: 979-8227713032

Written by Amarah Parks.

Table of Contents

I dedicate this book to the Light within and its incredible grace. Without it, this project may have never come to be. I also dedicate it to my two beautiful children, Luca and Arwen, who light up my days with sunshine. How blessed am I!

COURAGE
By: Amarah Parks

Chapter 1: A Spark

Refreshing cool winds of Flowerbud filled the air. The sun shone brilliantly on Alfalfa Hill, and countless little blossoms below soaked up those warm rays with gratitude. The Stream of Crashing Waters churned powerfully since the melted snow had joined its ranks, and the sunny bank was dotted with vibrant purple bellflowers. All in all, the hill was particularly abloom with a plethora of colors. Hive Honey Quest was nestled in the edge of Shadow Forest, the trees swaying lazily in the breeze. Winged creatures everywhere were singing their songs and filling the sky with music all around.

The world had been awakened quite early this year, bringing hope to every shivering creature. It had been a month now since Hive Honey Quest first emerged from the warmth of their home. While the effect of the New Beginning cult on top of other challenges was still actively being addressed every day, the memory of that dark time was quickly fading. In a short time, the hive was able to add greatly to their honey stores and recover from the long and trying cold season. Their bellies were full, and they were rejuvenated, with hope for a better future ahead.

The first thing to notice within the front of the landing grounds of the hive was the statue made in memory of Hope, Sweet Pea, and Thistle. The three were now regarded as heroes after so selflessly putting themselves in harm's way to protect Queen Royal and the hive from NB. If it weren't for them, things could have ended up very different.

Seated calmly next to the memorial were Courage, Iris, and Joy. Joy's heart was heavy at that moment. Firstly, she knew that Courage and Iris had both been very close with Thistle. They had become a trio of sorts, and the drone's absence clearly pained both of them deeply. But with the recent rehabilitation efforts being poured into former

New Beginning cult members, the two hadn't really had the chance to process the loss. Hive life had been a whirlwind. Secondly, she too felt the deep ache of loss for her late mentor, Sweet Pea. She had been such a thoughtful and kind teacher, and Joy had so appreciated her sweet nature.

Joy had just quietly joined the drones at the memorial moments earlier. She turned to her brother hesitantly, her gaze compassionate. "Hey brother," she buzzed in a low tone.

Her brother looked up at her with misty eyes. He hadn't noticed her joining them. "Sister, how are you?"

She looked at Courage and Iris silently. "I don't know... The hive isn't the same without them, is it?"

Iris responded quietly after a moment's pause. "No, no it isn't."

"Not at all. My only comfort is knowing that they wait for us in the beyond." Courage, while sad, reverberated with a deep sense of peace and acceptance.

"Yes, what a blessing!" Joy smiled weakly. But... I still miss them. They are greatly missed by many I think. It's amazing what incredible risks these bees took in order to serve the hive. They gave up everything to do what they believed was right, and in doing so, helped to save us all."

Iris looked guarded. "Nothing would have stopped Thistle from helping Hope. But I have to wonder why it was necessary to lose Thistle and Pea as well as her. I know they supported her within the cult, but their deaths seemed so unnecessary. It's hard to accept."

Joy sat still with the two drones, not speaking another word, and just remained in their mutual grieving. All she could think was how Sweet Pea was a gem, and she sure missed her. Pea often had mentioned Hope as well, who was a friend to her. Joy had gotten to know Hope through her mentor's occasional ramblings. The she-bee had been pivotal in bringing down New Beginning.

Several moments of reflection passed before she heard bees starting to gather around Queen Royal's podium. Curious, she stood and peered around the statue to hear her announcement.

After a few more minutes of assembly, Royal began. "Hello all! I hope you've enjoyed today's beautiful sunshine. I just have one announcement for you all. My dear little nurse bee Nectar has selected an apprentice to train. Meet Sugar!" The crowd cheered excitedly as Nectar and a young worker parted their way through to the podium. The young bee looked bright, smart, and warm. She carried herself with calmness and grace. Nectar proudly presented her apprentice to the observers before saying a few words.

"Thank you all! As you know, I am gaining in months. Sugar will be trained to take over my job in service to the Queen within just a few short weeks." She paused as the crowd clapped. "Along the same vein, any other young bees who would like to choose a more specialized focus in the hive should feel free to meet with some of the workers near the front. They represent the many specific roles a bee can take on here. And not just workers, but drones as well! There are many areas of work that you too may apply yourselves to. So please, explore the possibilities." The nurse bee stepped away from the podium.

"That's all for now!" The Queen buzzed joyfully and the crowd began to disperse.

Joy was enthralled. She had played the role of an ordinary bee for a while now, and a big part of her had always hoped to do something that excited her more one day. She paused to take a look back at Courage and Iris. She waved goodbye, letting her empathy show in her smile. Then, she shyly approached the line of bees who stayed to share their specialties.

She joined a small crowd of fresh-faced hive members who watched the teachers present. Not one talked over the other. It seemed like they were presenting their fields of work one by one. Joy had shown up just as an older she-bee was going into depth about her work as a Hive Planner.

"It's my job to figure out how things work best here. There needs to be a place for everyone, as well as space for each bee to do their job without interruption. I also get to help oversee things like cleaning and interior design. I help find artists to create things like the honeylamps you see in the royal cells. Essentially, this work is best for a bee who has natural talent in the areas of management, creativity, and social skills." The worker concluded, and another stepped forward.

"I'm an Undertaker bee. Simply put, I am the coroner for any and all bee deaths in the hive. I help arrange end-of-life services for loved ones, and I take care of the bodies. My job is simple, and can be emotionally challenging. The best candidate is someone who has a specific passion for comforting others and caring for those passed on." She gave a brief nod to indicate she was done.

A drone stepped forward next. "I am a Fighter! Anyone with an excitement for physical strength, incredible skill, and a fire to protect others is perfect for this job. Every bee learns basic fighting, but in this role, you would be leaders in war. You'd be well equipped to defend the hive against attack. Once training is established, you could do field work, or you could become a Hive Guard with regular and predictable shifts." He stepped back.

"As a Flower Specialist, you learn about the seasons and conditions in which flowers grow. You will know when the best and most plentiful nectar is available for each species. You will help initiate beedances to lead the hive to the best possible sources. If you have a passion for knowledge, nature, and good nectar, this is your thing!"

Joy sat quietly, listening to each bee present. *Everyone seems so passionate about their work. It's amazing!* Still, nothing seemed to click for her just yet. She continued to soak in each presentation, waiting for that spark. A nurse, a doctor, an adventurer, a scientist, and a maid all presented. Next, a middle aged worker began her speech.

"Do you have an unquenchable curiosity and a creative passion for protecting your loved ones? Then becoming an Enemy Researcher might just be your perfect fit. We spend our time observing and learning from possible threats, especially those of other species. When we gather enough information, we help guide inter-species interactions and dealings. While our title is "Enemy Researcher", we have also helped form inter-species alliances in the past. So if you are curious, driven, and want to help serve your hive in a meaningful way, consider this option."

Joy's face was alight. As other presenters continued speaking, she couldn't really hear them. She wasn't sure why, but the Enemy Researcher position had really awakened an excitement in her. *It sounds so unique and interesting! And, I could play an active role in protecting my home from any further grief.* With a decisive nod, she stepped forward to ask some questions. *I need to know more.*

Chapter 2: A Mysterious Gathering

The moon was as high as it was full. Dry leaves rustled in the chilly spring breeze. The sparsely vegetated land was dark, yet eerily illuminated with moonlight. Each projection from the ground cast long, formidable shadows everywhere. At the base of a large dead tree, dark shapes loomed and whispered amongst themselves. They stood huddled together in the shadows out of sight. After waiting for quite some time, one spoke up.

"Szzhouldn't zey be hzere by now?"

The question caused a disruption in the group before their leader hissed. "*Quietzzzz!*"

Just moments later, a group of dark shapes came into sight and approached the dead tree. The creatures waited in anticipation as they tried to make out who was coming near. Before long, their leader partially emerged from the protection of the tree's shadow to greet the mysterious newcomers.

"Greetings, Hissgaar," the leader of the guests buzzed curtly. He was a bit smaller than the shadow creatures, but he was the tallest of his group. He held himself with confidence and resolve.

"Greetingzzzz." Hissgaar paced in front of the newcomer. "What wazzz zee holdup?" He demanded with an edge in his tone.

"Horseflies," He huffed. "Not dangerous of course, but a nuisance. I didn't want anyone following us here, so I took a winding path."

A strange sound emanated from the group of creatures. It was between a hiss, buzz, and chortle. It wasn't clear if it were the sound of disapproval, a sort of laughter, or something else. After the creatures quieted, Hissgaar flashed a menacing smile. "Puny scoundrelzzz. But not a tzzerrible szznack! Zzey know not to szzhow up around herezzz."

The newcomers appeared shaken by the strange laughter and response. Their leader was not phased, however. "Let us discuss the terms and negotiations."

"Yesszzz, review the termzzz."

"One of us each month for a year, or twelve of us total at any time you wish upon completion. In addition, all our dead or exiled will be delivered to you fresh for a year. There will be means to get them to you even in the coldest months if you wish."

The creatures began laughing terribly again. "Twelvzze? Zzzat izzz a total rip-offzzz. We needzz at leaszzzt triple." The group cheered.

The leader stood quietly.

"Izzz not your group mighty and szzztrong?"

"We can uphold double, a total of 24, given that no more than three will be expected in the first three months. We have plans to multiply our brood, but everyone else is quite needed to put the plan into motion."

The creature brooded and buzzed silently as he contemplated. "I can acczept this... only of courzzzse, if you can provide zzzomething much more valuable azzz well. A producing honey bee queen."

Hissgaar's words caused a quiet ripple of buzzing through the small crowd of newcomers. They were appalled by his tall ask, as a honey bee queen was worth a great sum. They themselves sought a queen, and hadn't found one after several months of searching. Still, their leader stood tall and unwavering. "We can promise you a queen within 3 months. We will decide when the queen is provided within that time frame."

"Weee will notzz fightzzz until a queen izzz provided." The creature stared with fiery eyes.

After much deliberation, the leader responded. "Fair enough. I will see to it."

Hissgaar smiled with a terrible glee, clapping. "Pleazzze, let usszz szzhow you our nest azz arranged. Obzzerve the szzztrength of our rankzzz."

Silently, everyone began filing toward the trunk of the dead tree. Hissgaar and his group had split up to surround the newcomers on both ends. From a slanted gash slightly off of the ground, a dull green glow emanated. They were led up and into the green gash. The newcomers had never been inside the nest before, and there was a trace of fear on their faces despite attempts to conceal it. Their leader maintained a strong front, angrily nudging his comrades to recover their senses.

The nest was constructed with compacted layers of a paper-like material. The green glow became more obvious, and the overall feel of the nest was menacing and strange. There were countless narrow hallways that wound with no apparent pattern. Now and then, they reached a wider opening. One of such rooms, the newcomers gasped as they saw various fireflies carrying out chores and tasks. To each, a long strand of dead grasses braided together was tethered. The fireflies looked sickly and unusually dim compared to how they would appear in nature. They moved slowly.

"Szzome of our szzlavezzz." Hissgar gestured forth proudly. "Zzey are terrible food, but good lightingzz and very obedientzz."

Another of Hissgaar's bunch mumbled to the newcomers, adding, "Zheeeyyy die, five a dzzayy. We replace zzzhem azzz zhey go. We hazz fifty at a tzzime. Zzheyyy taste yucky. Honey beezzzz taste much betterzzz." The creature stared at them, licking his chops. "Weezz wanted a honey beezzz brood for szzzoooo long!"

The crew of visitors stayed close together. Many looked clearly shaken and appalled at what they were seeing. But their leader stayed level, and they continued the tour through the nest. After maybe an hour of observing the inner workings of the nest and being in Hissgaar's company, the leader cleared his throat.

COURAGE

"Hissgaar, I am glad we've come to a mutually beneficial agreement, and have seen your home. Now we will be on our way. Our next meeting, as previously agreed upon, will be at the rosebush in a week. Let's plan for the same day and time as now. We will be in touch weekly for the time being as our plans grow and commence."

With a few farewells and awkward pleasantries, the newcomers were escorted to the nest's entrance so they could be on their way. They slipped into the darkness with a sigh of relief. Before long they disappeared into the horizon, just as the chill of night was giving way to the warm rays of the sun.

Chapter 3: Third and Final Prophecy

Sugar and Nectar stood together around a table full of herbs. Sugar had just begun training to become Hive Honey Quest's nurse bee successor, and her brain was already exploding with the information.

"See, the three core callings of a nurse bee are the following: Sanctuary, Insight, and Medicine. Sanctuary has to do with having empathy, emotional maturity, and great compassion towards others, especially those who you are in care of. Insight refers to our deeper spiritual connection. We pursue the Light so that we may relay its message and offer guidance to the Queen. And Medicine has to do with our broad knowledge of healing, herbs, treatments, and medical care. Before us is every herb you can find locally that has medicinal value. You will learn their uses and applications. All of this information will be accessible to you in writing, but you should strive to learn it by heart as soon as you can."

Sugar looked up to see the callings on the wall next to a few other significant writings.

<u>The Three Core Callings of a Nurse Bee</u>
Sanctuary: Empathy, Compassion, Emotional Maturity
Insight: Spiritual Connection, Faith, Guidance for the Queen
Medicine: Healing, Knowledge, Herbs, Treatments

"Nectar, you've told me a lot about the Honeycrystal. How often does a fully-fledged nurse bee go there?" Sugar was always full of questions, and secretly preferred this topic over the herbs.

Nectar paused. "At first, I was going at least weekly. But soon, Lighthive started to become as present as I am to you. When you reach that level of closeness, you won't often require the Honeycrystal, but you will still love it. Now, I find myself there around once a month, or maybe twice. Often it's when I am seeking guidance on specific concerns." Turning back to the table of herbs, she opened her mouth to speak.

"Why did you choose me, Nectar?" Sugar asked.

Nectar took a breath, giving Sugar a sideways glance. "Lighthive chose you. I knew because of the vibrations I felt within my abdomen. You are filled with compassion, a hard-working nature, and a curiosity for the Light. You have not just a curiosity, but also a natural inclination towards it." She paused again. "Now, it's time to learn these herbs."

The day dragged on and on as Nectar presented all that she knew about herbs. While it wasn't Sugar's most exciting endeavor, many things proved to be fascinating. Chamomile, when mashed or soaked in water, had various applications including reducing inflammation and promoting skin healing. It could even help with digestion. Sugar knew she'd be needing the books as her reference for a long time, though. There were far too many details to memorize in one sitting - or even several.

Toward the end of the day while Nectar was talking about lavender, someone interrupted them. There was an urgent knock at the door. "Nectar?" A drone's voice rang.

Nectar jumped. "It's Courage, hive mentor. He must need something." She opened the door, and the tall, handsome drone walked into the room swiftly. "What is it, Courage?"

"I... heard something you need to hear. One of my messengers delivered it to me in a dream." He glanced around sheepishly. "I may have taken an afternoon nap."

"Do tell!" Nectar pulled out some chairs for the three of them to sit. The drone looked pretty ruffled. Sugar was sure his message wasn't going to be all sunshine and butterflies.

"Okay, so this is what I heard." He cleared his throat.

"A dark shadow follows,
As evil ancestors rise,
They gather with danger,

Hidden by moonlit skies.
Revenge is their friend,
And darkness their ally,
They seek the end,
And a new world nigh.
They wait now,
Eager to strike with terrible force.
To steal and plunder,
And plot their course.
A final precipice
Before true and lasting peace."

Sugar gasped. This message was a truly ominous riddle. Nectar was quiet and deep in thought. Several moments passed as the three sat silently, letting it soak in.

"Do you think this means...?" Courage didn't finish his sentence.

"Perhaps." Nectar spoke, her voice curious. "We can't know for sure. But I have a very specific feeling about this. What is coming will be our greatest feat, but can bring us the peace we have longed for. A complete and lasting peace. This feels like a closing chapter."

Courage sighed. "Well, at least there's one silver lining." After a moment's pause, he regarded the teacher and student. "I feel like our hive is going to be vulnerable. This is a time of transition. Even the queen grows old." His voice was somber.

Nectar looked at him. "Yes, we will be. Since you hold a position of leadership here and have many bees' trust, I have a feeling you will play a big role in our preparations. Perhaps that's why Lighthive gave this prophecy to you. You are quite special, Courage." The small nurse bee's eyes twinkled with awe.

Dipping his head with humility, Courage grunted quietly in acknowledgement before turning toward the door. "I'll stay receptive to whatever role Lighthive will have me fill." Then, the drone slipped out of the room.

Nectar remained silent, her expression thoughtful and curious. Sugar stayed quiet too at first, but after fifteen slow minutes she spoke. "What are you thinking about, Nectar?"

The old nurse bee smiled at her apprentice. "Many things. Courage has always fascinated me. In particular, something he said today has piqued my interest."

"That prophecy no doubt?"

"No, though that is also to be carefully regarded. Actually, when he came in, he said: 'One of my messengers delivered it to me in a dream.' Firstly, it's a rare occurrence for most bees to meet with a messenger in a dream and make it sound so nonchalant. He is used to meeting with Lighthive in his dreams. Secondly, he said 'one' of his messengers. From what I've seen in my years, no bee has ever had more than one messenger. In fact, a messenger is really just a way of communication with the Light. There would be no need for multiples."

"What does that mean then?" Sugar was intrigued.

"I don't know. Perhaps he is able to meet with ancestors of late. That would explain him having more than one 'messenger'. If that's the case, he is a rare kind of bee. Most bees never get to speak with their ancestors even once. When it *has* occurred, it's been a one-time sentimental type vision or dream. But he meets with them regularly."

Sugar ruminated in all of this. "You seem very curious about Courage. Why don't you just ask him who he is or why he's different?"

Nectar frowned. "While asking that sort of thing isn't necessarily wrong, it's just not my way. I trust that whatever I must know will be made known to me, and that I'm not entitled to know the spiritual life of others. It's intimate and worth protecting." She flashed a little smile. "But I sure enjoy putting together the mysterious puzzle of curiosity!"

Sugar smiled. Her mentor's exceedingly patient and kind nature never failed to warm her heart, but she was different from Nectar. She wasn't afraid to ask questions and gather information. Perhaps she would do just that next time she ran into the mysterious drone. Shaking her wings, she took a breath. "I assume we must relay the prophecy to the Queen at once."

"Yes, yes." Nectar acted as if she were roused from a dream at the realization. "Of course! We will go to her right away."

Sugar laughed. "I can't believe that after hearing that dark and looming poem, all you could think about was Courage's mysteries."

"Nothing seems to phase me anymore. Besides, there never was a single thing gained from worrying. But action? Yes. We will do our best to decipher the prophecy and reap the benefit it offers. It'll guide our preparations. But as we know it, hive life must go on as usual until the storm arrives. In fact, it's even more pertinent that we do so, since there is much to be done!"

Sugar refrained from asking more questions, even though she still had so many. *What has to be done? Who is this dark enemy? Will I be able to carry the baton when Nectar is gone? Will I be ready? Who is Courage? How had Nectar found this peace which stands as solid as a mountain no matter what is going on around her?* But instead, she let them bounce around her brain unanswered, and consciously decided to try Nectar's way. She took a breath and let her boundless thoughts go unanswered. It was hard at first to settle them, but then it was... exciting. She felt especially present and observant of the world around her. A spark of curiosity and wonder sparkled within, and it made the present moment feel especially vibrant and awesome. *I'm not Nectar, but I am sure honored to train under her.*

Chapter 4: The Next Chapter

Royal and Sting sat together quietly, gazing at a certain cluster of brood comb. The King's face was filled with emotions of every kind. Pride, sadness, excitement, and heartbreak. "I hate that I may have to exist in a world without you." He shuddered.

Royal rested her head on his shoulder. The queen had aged. While still vibrant, she knew full well that her time was coming. She was producing less eggs than ever and could feel Lighthive calling her home soon. The Queen hadn't informed the hive yet, but change was coming. She smiled sadly, a tear escaping her eye. "My love, you have brought such beauty to my life. You have been strong when I was stumbling. You loved and supported me through the most challenging phases of my existence. Beyond that, you have been a place of abundant joy and friendship, making me a better queen." She turned to look into his eyes. "You are honorable and faithful to the Light. I could have never imagined a better King."

Sting looked at her with deep affection. "You have awakened me to my full potential. You have honored me and elevated me to positions of respect. I am a better drone because of your love, and I am in awe of you every day. Thank you. Thank you for everything you are and the grace you have shown me." He lowered his head, crying. "Life has meant so much more with you by my side."

The two held each other as they looked down at the brood. Four pupae were growing in large, unusual brood cells. With each was a generous helping of a special formula called royal jelly. The four females would soon hatch as mature queens, and would then compete to win the place of leadership in the hive. There would be competitions of wit, merit, and character. By the end, one Queen and her chosen mate would be selected to fill Royal's shoes. The other three would leave the hive to potentially grow something new elsewhere. While it would be an exciting time, it would also be bittersweet. It would be vulnerable too, as a brand new Queen settled in to her position of responsibility.

"What do you think of the prophecy?" Royal buzzed after a time of silence.

"Buzzz. I think it tells of Buzzz returning. We have all been aware that his survival was possible after the War of the Ghost, but of course we hoped it wouldn't be true. After about six months, who knows what kind of army he's been able to build. We need to prepare for the worst."

Royal nodded, troubled. "I agree. He is charismatic and sharp. We should inform our allies soon about this possibility, and keep the hive busy with training. I only regret that I might not be able to oversee this fight."

"You have done the hard work to get us this far, my dear. And as Nectar shared, I believe the end of this threat will mean a season of true peace and freedom. Our children will live in a golden age thanks to your bravery."

"And yours." The Queen buzzed. "Look at our daughters wiggling around." The two smiled down at the brood, a glint of hope and pride in their eyes. The King kissed his mate's cheek, and they sat in peace for a while longer.

JOY WAITED PATIENTLY as a crowd gathered around the podium where Royal stood. Once enough bees were present, the Queen began speaking. "Today's is a huge announcement. As you can probably sense, the hive is approaching a time of change. I'd like to announce that in a week's time, four young queens will emerge from their combs ready to win the crown." The crowd rippled in a mixture of concern and excitement. "I feel my days as Queen are reaching their end. Soon, a new Queen will lead with a new nurse bee at her side. The Queen Games are an exciting series of events to witness, and will help the hive leadership decide who is best fit to lead Hive Honey Quest. In the meantime, I'd like to refresh every hive member's abilities in the area of self-defense, and those of you who have a specialty should focus your efforts into that with intensity. It is my responsibility to make you aware that a threat could be looming." Gasps shuddered through the crowd. "We have no solid evidence or sightings, but we have received a new prophecy meant to prepare us. So prepare we shall! Speak to your mentors and group leaders for specific instructions on how you are to prepare in your specialty. This threat is not here yet, and we still have time. So as this week passes, *do* get excited about the games! They will be great fun. Public opinions will be heard as we consider a new queen, so we hope you'll be a part of the process. That is all!"

As the crowd broke, whispering and muttering all sorts of concerns, Joy stood still. Her heart felt confused with emotions. She was deeply sad. Yet, there was such a brilliant glimmer of hope and excitement that resided as well.

Ever since she began training into a specialty a few days ago, she had felt inspired. Royal's command to delve further into her specialty was very exciting. *I need to ask my unit leader how we will proceed.* Until now, her studies had only been extremely introductory. She'd heard some fascinating stories from history about various species and their involvement with the hive, whether good or bad. But she was eager to begin learning the skills rather than just hearing stories about them.

The unit leader for 'Enemy Researchers' was the same middle-aged worker who had presented the specialty a few days before. This particular group was not a large one. Joy was one of perhaps only a hundred students, and some were in even more niche specialties studying only certain species. There were a few others who helped teach and lead, but the unit leader - called Verity - would be the one to ask.

Joy searched for the worker, peering through the crowd. She spotted small gatherings of bees forming at the edges of the landing grounds. After finally spotting Verity, she flew toward the small group with haste.

"Okay, enough of us have gathered to spread the news to the others." Verity began, Joy just within earshot. "It's time for the new students to get into the field. Older students may lead groups to study certain species and their behaviors first-hand. Continue to lead these groups until every new student has studied each species from the list I'm presenting. Willow, take some to learn about flies and horseflies. Grace, you lead studies on spiders. Creed, you can teach on mammals such as skunks and bears, then alternate to frogs. Tansy, please teach on hive pests such as mites and moths. Keep that course short and switch off with birds of the air. The last four categories are unlikely to present as allies in war, but it's still important to get an introduction. And finally, Oak, take out groups to learn about wasps, hornets, and ants. Such social insects are most likely to present a threat to us when it comes to enemy alliances. These types are easier to communicate with, and easier to find agreeable terms with."

Verity finished speaking and gestured for groups to form. Joy didn't mind which one she started with since she was excited to learn about all of them. But based on where she was standing, Oak's group gathered the nearest. She joined the fringes, if a bit shyly. About ten bees had taken their place beside Oak. Joy tried to remember the category Oak was leading. After a few moments, the sturdy drone cleared his voice.

"Fellow ERs, let's begin the studies of the order Hymenoptera, of which we are a part." The old drone had a particularly deep and weathered voice. "We will study the family Vespidae, which includes wasps, hornets, and yellowjackets, and the family Formicidae, which includes many kinds of ants. This area of study is quite large, and especially important. As Verity stated, these insect groups are the easiest for us to communicate with. They tend to run social societies much like ours in concept. Most members of these families are formidable natural predators of honey bees. To start off our learning,

I will take you to an abandoned hornet's nest we have discovered. We will need to be careful, as hornets have been sighted taking materials from the nest to reuse. Let's be off!"

Feeling exhilarated and intrigued, Joy took off along with the group. They filed out of the hive entrance into the forest. Though most of the farm property was north and west of the hive, they headed southeast at top speed. The forest continued pretty thickly for quite some time as they zipped past. After about 15 minutes, they had flown approximately 5 miles. They began to slow as the bright edge of the forest came into sight. Joy tried to catch her breath after the jaunt, and the group coasted a bit to the left along the inside edge of the trees.

Before long, Joy spotted it. A giant mass with a paper-like texture hung delicately on one of the taller branches of a mature red pine. It was old and tattered, with some of its material ripped away from its form. It was obvious to spot beneath the sparse spring foliage.

The group approached cautiously, Oak at the head. He looked skilled and nimble, as though he had encountered the foes before. He seemed to know exactly how to proceed. The group carefully adhered to his silent commands using symbols they had been introduced to just yesterday. When it was clear that there was no danger, Oak spoke.

"We are safe to proceed, and to speak aloud." They were just feet away from the mass now. It was about a foot long and a foot tall, looming and egg-shaped. "As you can see, this large abode is constructed of a paper-like material. Hornets actually chew wood and mix it with their saliva to create this solution. It is then often recycled the next year. Hornets use their nest for one warm season before completely dying out each winter. The only hornets to survive the cold are the queens, who hibernate. This nest probably housed close to 700 workers in its prime. While this number is nothing compared to our ranks, hornets are capable of stinging as many times as they want to without death. Another oddity is that this nest hasn't been totally recycled. Therefore, we have reason to believe that the members of this nest have been completely eradicated, and it has simply been scavenged here and there. Still, even though it is late into the spring, we are always careful when approaching it."

Joy was soaking in the new information with an attention only passion can create. Where most bees would naturally forget half or more of the facts stated one time, her brain was truly absorbing almost every word. Joy was so excited to have discovered this purpose, and to have a clear direction ahead. *Somehow, I am going to help Hive Honey Quest using this knowledge.*

Chapter 5: Developments

Courage sighed deeply. He had just completed his last mentoring session for the day, and it had been quite intense. For the very first time, Theo had booked with him.

Theo, brother of the late Thistle, had a complicated past. Not only had he been a dedicated member of New Beginning, but he had spent much of his life serving as Buzzz's right hand drone. He expended most of his efforts in life trying to rise in status and respect, things he craved with intensity. After NB's fall, he was left aimless again, and hadn't a shred of confidence or drive.

Despite persistent efforts, it had taken weeks to get Theo to consider a mentoring session. The stubborn drone didn't seem to like talking, especially not about vulnerable things. But Courage was determined to get through to him.

"Theo! I'm glad to see you." Courage had buzzed welcomingly.

Theo had grunted as a response, like an old creature who didn't want to be disturbed.

"How are things?" Courage asked.

Theo sat rigid in a protective stance, almost glaring at the younger drone from his chair. It took a long moment for him to give any answers. Drawing a long breath, he buzzed gruffly. "Pretty bland. Nothing to do, nothing to live for."

Courage searched his face, waiting for him to expound. He didn't. *Tough to crack...* "Tell me about The War of the Ghost. I wasn't there to witness it."

Confused, the gruff drone shifted in his chair. "Well, that was a long time ago. I was right under Buzzz, helping to lead his troops. The tides changed and the resistance was winning. I betrayed Buzzz toward the end." The drone began to loosen up a little, suddenly recalling certain events and memories from that time. Courage simply listened and watched as Theo lit up. He was the most animated when recalling times that he had been highly respected or honored. With a few short responses, Courage kept him engaged until he appeared much more relaxed and comfortable.

"You were made to lead, huh?" Courage offered.

"Born for it! No one has my vigor or dedication!" Theo buzzed excitedly.

"What is the most important trait in a leader?"

Theo paused, his expression changing from confident to uncertain. "I suppose... strength. A good leader is strong and unwavering."

Courage smiled. "That's a good one." He remained silent for a while, studying Theo's face.

"Well... what do you think?" Theo offered uncomfortably.

"I think the most important trait in a leader is humility."

Theo scoffed. "Nah. Humility is too soft. That's the way to get trampled."

"No! Humility is the greatest show of strength there is. A good leader is confident in his way, but is always seeking suggestions from his followers. He knows that he doesn't always have it figured out, and that other perspectives offer the chance for a more complete and perfect leadership."

Theo's face was twisted in criticism. "I've never seen such a leader."

"How about Royal and Sting?"

Theo sighed. "The Monarch berated their leadership because she wanted to take over. She needed to convince others that she was the rightful queen. But ultimately, their leadership has been... good enough, I suppose."

Courage had been intrigued by Theo's answer. The drone clearly had a mind of his own. This session wouldn't be about NB rehabilitation, but rather about getting to this drone's heart. He spoke again. "The best leaders recognize that their position warrants a great deal of caution. When one is in power, they are responsible for the well being of so many others. It weighs heavily on any good leader. Because of this, those most fit for leadership often don't seek it out themselves. Rather, they are often elected or sometimes even born into it."

It seemed that Theo's walls went right up again. He sighed, rolling his eyes. "Don't demean me with your big words."

"Well that's not my intention, certainly!" Courage raised his eyebrows.

"I might talk simple, but I'm sharper than you think. You imply that my desire to lead means I'm not fit for it." The drone stood up, seemingly ready to leave.

"I think you have many natural leadership qualities, but you also have other motivations besides serving those who follow you. If those lesser motivations would step aside, you'd be kingly."

Theo paused. He was angry and visibly trembling, but his expression betrayed a slight consideration for Courage's words.

"All you need now is humility. You don't always have to be on guard. Lay it down, and be real."

The drone hesitated, clenching his jaw. "I have never done that before." His eyes were cast downward.

Courage said nothing for a bit, allowing for some silence. Slowly, he stirred. "I think we've had enough for one session. Let's meet again in a week."

Hesitantly, the drone nodded and wrote himself into the appointment book. He then left the room without a word.

Courage contemplated Theo's situation. The drone had been born and raised in a tyrannical hive. His only two options seemed to be: submit and be lowly, or strive for excellence and be notable. Theo had been extremely successful at that. But beneath it all, he had his own mind. His mind had never been lorded over by anyone else, just his own shortcomings. That had to indicate a sort of strength. *No doubt he suffered a lot of abuse.* The drone had been hardened by life. But deep down, he was not cruel or twisted. *There may be hope for him yet.* Courage sighed sanguinely.

IN A DARK, SPACIOUS cell, Buzzz sat brooding. He did this often, but this time was different.

A couple months ago, Buzzz's outlook point near Hive Honey Quest had sighted a small group of bees leaving the hive just before dark. Thinking they could be used as an offering to approach potential allies, the drones who spotted them had promptly taken them hostage to the warmth of the base. There had been a couple drones and some workers. The self-proclaimed leader of the bunch had vehemently declared her significance as an attempt to save their lives. She had led a group within the hive called New Beginning, and claimed to be capable of laying viable eggs. Considering this too unusual to be hasty, Buzzz had decided to keep Sun and ordered for all the other refugees to be used for trade and negotiations as originally planned.

Buzzz's quest for a honeybee queen had been unsuccessful for so long. But when Sun arrived, a small seed of hope had grown. Perhaps she would be able to produce a queen much sooner than they had planned. Maybe she would be as good as a queen on her own. But unfortunately, the experiment was failing.

Thelytoky, bah! Buzzz sighed in frustration. Standing up from his seat, he walked decidedly to one corner of his cell. He undid the lock on the outside and entered the much smaller cell.

Sun was basking pathetically on her thin cushion, groaning. "Buzzz!" She jumped, surprised.

Sun had been a pain to keep. She was used to being elevated and respected, but there was no room for that here. Buzzz was the leader, and he had decided to test Sun's abilities by his own terms. She had been reduced to a lowly servant, and she hadn't taken the adjustment lightly. She required constant correction, and even still, always operated with defiance.

"I've come to check on the larvae."

Sun appeared instantly rigid. "They aren't ready yet!" Instead of her usual difficult nature, her voice was laced with something else. Fear?

Sun was not nearly as fruitful as a queen, but she had managed to lay enough eggs to fill a tiny shelf of comb. Since her arrival, maybe ten drones and five workers had hatched. All had been unsatisfactory to Buzzz in both size and form, being a bit smaller. They had gone to be used for negotiations, despite Sun's disapproval. But now, Buzzz had ordered the making of a few queens. A queen could have already produced thousands of offspring, and his patience was growing thin. Even still, the queens Sun produced might not be acceptable either.

Buzzz went straight to the few meager rows of comb expectantly. It had been more than two weeks since laying, which meant that the queens should be ready to emerge from their unique cells. He peered at the protuberances impatiently. There was no translucence to see through due to the unique construction of queen cells. Suddenly and without warning, he tore at the entrance of one with vigor.

Sun let out a huge gasp as this, scrambling to her feet. "What are you doing?!" She tugged at Buzzz's leg with all of her strength. He tossed her away with ease.

"They are ready enough to come out. I'm going to see once and for all if you are of any worth to me." Sun wept pathetically on the floor while he swiftly removed the cap of a queen cell. A young bee's head became visible, and the creature stirred uncomfortably at the disturbance. In very little time, Buzzz reached in and yanked the young she-bee out of the comb and onto the floor.

The bee was small and unpromising as she slowly came to life. Dazed, she blinked and began to move every part of her body one by one. Buzzz stared down at her, merciless and with a skeptical eye. The bee seemed to have the mark of fertility, being different from a worker bee. However, she looked a bit underdeveloped, similar to Sun. Maybe it was just that she didn't have the characteristic size and strength that Hive Honey Quest had acquired with time. She was average, and on the low end at that. The young queen slowly collected herself onto her feet, coming to her full size. "Hello?" She blinked in confusion.

Buzzz stood in front of her, waving his antennae in front of her eyes. She didn't respond to the gesture in any way, and continued to look about blankly. "Blind?" He turned to Sun, furious. "You produce all kinds of useless stock!"

Sun trembled, petrified. "I... I..." She dragged herself toward her pillow in a pointless attempt to escape Buzzz's wrath.

"I don't see a need for you anymore. We'll see what we can make of these queens, if anything, but none of them will fit to offer to Hissgaar. We are back to square one. So much time wasted." He scoffed, seizing Sun by the scruff of her thorax to remove her from the room without mercy.

Chapter 6: So It Begins

Sugar's thoughts were spinning as she rested in her cell. She and Nectar had spent the day focusing on the second core calling of a nurse bee: Insight. Part of developing her spiritual connection with Lighthive meant visiting the Honeycrystal. So, after a morning of instruction and book work, they had taken off for the Mountain of the Sun.

The journey there had been extremely interesting to Sugar. Her spiritually sensitive mind had drawn many theories for the significance of things. For example, the friendly path through the wild hive's territory, signifying that those who seek Lighthive are a family. The gorgeous valley, a gem to behold, revealed the perfection and magnetic draw of faith. The battering wind and difficult climb to the tunnels indicated perhaps that it is not always easy to strive for the Light. It may feel uncomfortable or even impossible at times. The network of dark tunnels, implying that one's path can easily be lost if they do not watch carefully for the Light.

Sugar's entrance into the dream-like state was shocking, but invigorating. In the golden forest, she had felt like she was exactly where her heart longed to be. It was home. Every winged creature lived together in harmony, and there was nothing but goodness. She had met her guide, of sorts. Her messenger was a noble owl who went by the name of Softwing. She was almost painfully graceful. When she spoke, it felt like her voice created rays of gentle golden light.

Sugar knew deep down that Softwing was just a mouthpiece for the Light. She was someone Sugar could relate to and interact with. But the Light itself? How glorious it must be to behold. And slowly, Sugar decided that she wanted to truly *know* that Light intimately.

Softwing had taken her around a bit, and spoken to her about many things. But all that Sugar could truly absorb at that moment was the great peace she had felt. Both peace and inspiration together. She wanted to go back to that golden forest every day.

Nectar had told her afterwards, "Bees like you and I are likely to have more dreams and interactions with Lightive than others. We have been given a larger measure of faith. It's a gift. You could dream of it every night in some seasons of life."

Sugar was so excited. It was this part of being a nurse bee that she had looked the most forward to. It awakened her very being, and gave her such powerful purpose that she was content to revel in. *Everything I do will be for Lighthive.* She smiled. *Even memorizing herbs.*

She was now splayed out on her cushion, too excited to try for a nap. Yet, to dream of Lighthive was all she wanted to do. As she was thinking this, a whisper came to her conscience.

"Wherever you are, I am not far from you."

Sugar gasped. She knew what this meant. It wasn't purely meant as a comfort, but also a conviction. While she loved the euphoric feelings she'd had at the Honeycrystal, she knew that it wasn't all about living on those highs alone. She was to live present each day, tuning in to the quiet voice that lived within her. Her excitement changed from a childish wonder to a deep appreciation. *I am never alone, and you are always watching. Every day is a day with you. Help me to do the right things, and even the hard things, for you.*

Something bumped into Sugar, jolting her out of her trance-like introspection. She became presently aware and heard the bustle of crowds around her. *Oh, I'm in the landing grounds. I must have zoned out on the way here.* Queen Royal had called for an important meeting this evening for the whole hive to attend. Sugar looked around in awe. She had never seen so many of her hivemates in one place at one time. Her mind could not fathom the number, but it had to be tens of thousands. Just then, the crowd grew considerably quiet, and Sugar looked to see Royal making her way to the podium.

Nectar was standing beside the Queen, peering into the crowd with a searching expression. When the nurse bee's eyes settled on Sugar, she gestured for her to come up as well. *Right, of course!* Sugar still wasn't completely used to standing up front with the Queen. Thankfully, she was near to the front. She carefully shouldered her way through the tightly-packed crowd, making her way to Nectar. It was no small feat.

"Sugar, this is a special time. It's even more important now for you to stand with me than ever."

Sugar didn't have time to process her mentor's words before Royal began to speak. "Welcome one and all!" The elegant old queen was the picture of grace, and her face shone with pride as she looked upon her offspring. "As I have updated you on previously, my time as the Queen is coming to an end. It all becomes very real today." She paused dramatically. "Your four young queens who will compete for my title have emerged from the nursery comb this afternoon!"

The hive exploded into excited buzzing. Hive members in the middle of the crowd passed the information to the bees behind them until the whole hive heard. The commotion lasted for a minute or two.

Sugar was excited. She knew that this moment had been long approaching, but it hadn't sunken in yet. The time was coming when the new queen would be selected. This affected everybee of course, but it was even more monumental for her. The next queen would be the leader that Sugar would be the closest to. She would spend all of her days aiding and advising her, and keeping her in good health. Sugar truly hoped that whoever was selected would be as kind and amazing as Royal. *What happens if we don't get along?* She didn't want to imagine what life might be like in that scenario. *I wonder how the young queen is chosen.*

Royal finally continued as the crowd relaxed. "These four queens will partake in various tests of physical, mental, and spiritual capability.

In the end, her selection will be decided by hive leadership. That being said, we seek your participation as well. Those who are able to attend the Queen Games will be asked to vote on a successor, as well as stating the trait they see in her that is most valuable. The voting will help guide us in our final decision. The leaders who will make the final decision include myself, King Sting, Nectar, Courage, and Sugar."

Sugar tilted her head. *Wow, that's a big responsibility. But also, I'm glad I'll have a say in whose right hand bee I'll remain for the rest of my life!*

"The Games will begin promptly tomorrow. We will start with the physical games. There will be fun agility competitions to watch, and an evaluation to ensure all queens are fit for laying eggs. The following two days will include the other categories of tests and games. In addition to their prowess in these competitions, we will also observe them to decide if their attitude, approach, and skillset are what this hive needs. And now..." Royal paused again, building anticipation in the crowd. "Meet the four contenders."

Royal stepped aside and gestured behind her. In a few seconds, the four she-bees came into view. They were all tall and strong in stature, and radiant and lively in countenance. Each face was alight with some combination of emotions. Nervousness, hope, determination, shyness, resolve, pride, humility, fear, optimism, and too many more to count. Overall though, they were quite similar in presentation, and there was no way to know each queen's personality at a glance.

"The ladies! They have accepted the following names and competition numbers: Crystal (1), Amethyst (2), Blossom (3), and Amber (4). After our queen is selected from the lot, the three remaining queens will leave the hive to possibly start their own legacies. When they each go, some of you may choose to join them if you'd like to help secure their futures. The departing queens will be able to establish their own hives, whether a few miles away, or a hundred miles." Royal let all the information sink in for a moment. "They may even choose a drone to bring along." She smiled. "Well, that is all for tonight! Rest well, and be ready for the days of festivities to begin first thing tomorrow!"

Sugar watched as the giant crowd started to disperse, buzzing energetically. Turning back to Royal and the young queens, she smiled nervously. Nectar nudged her. "Come, let's meet the younglings."

They quietly approached the queens as Royal spoke with them. "Your cells are all ready for you. You'll be staying separately, of course. In most hives, the rivalry between young queens is immense. But here, you will all earn a fair chance, and be given the opportunity of a life even if you don't win the title. There will be absolutely no use of stingers here." Royal smiled in a joking manner, but Sugar knew that she needed to say it. In most hives, whichever queen emerged first would make sure that no other queen could come out to challenge her. It was the way of nature, but Hive Honey Quest often tried to do things differently than the rest.

Royal turned to welcome Nectar and Sugar. "This is Nectar, my dear little nurse bee, and her apprentice, Sugar. Impressing these two may be your most important task. A queen's nurse bee is her closest confidante, and Sugar will be assigned to Hive Honey Quest's next queen. A queen only has two or three of such helpers in a lifetime, and the bond between you is extremely important. More on that later."

The young queens greeted Sugar one-by-one with a respectful nod. Sugar waved and smiled shyly. "Hi. I wish each of you the best of luck in the Queen Games!" She offered, trying to sound confident. They smiled respectfully before Royal led them away to their individual cells.

Nectar's face was thoughtful. She gestured for Sugar to follow her away from the podium, not speaking. They headed toward the room Sugar received most of her instruction in.

"What's on your mind?" Sugar asked, being always slightly less comfortable with long silences than Nectar apparently was. Or maybe, just slightly more curious.

Nectar smiled. "There are always things to wonder about, Sugar. What an exciting and mysterious time we get to partake in now!" She paused. "And what an exciting moment for you!"

"I think I'm more nervous than excited!" Sugar buzzed.

"Well, life is full of risks. But because of Lighthive, we know that whatever comes our way can ultimately be used for our good. What peace that brings!"

Sugar stared at her mentor in admiration. She possessed such an unshakable zest for the wonder of life. Uncertainty didn't scare her. She took everything in stride, and had the skill to handle whatever came her way. "How will I ever fill your shoes?" Sugar was a bit surprised by what came out of her own mouth.

Nectar turned to her, serious. "You won't. My shoes won't fit you. You'll have your very own pair."

"Huh?" Sugar buzzed.

"You and I are completely different creations! And I know that you will be amazing and unique in your own way. You were made to be the next nurse bee."

Sugar blushed under her mentor's praise. "I only wish I could fast-forward. I'm bound to make mistakes along the way. I'd rather be fully equipped and avoid failure."

Nectar smiled. "Again, ALL of the things you say and do will shape you and your future. But with the Light, even your mistakes can turn into good later on. That's the beauty of it. Trust me, you are made to do this."

Chapter 7: The Queen Games

The competitors are as follows:
Crystal (1)
Amethyst (2)
Blossom (3)
Amber (4)

The Queen Games were a huge ordeal. Early risers spent the morning plotting agility tests - both indoor and outdoor. The indoor course was smaller and closer quartered, and the queens were not to fly in its bounds. It was more about footwork, speed, and agility. Outside, the course was huge and spacious, incorporating navigational talent and flight maneuvers. It would be more of a test of endurance and skill. The bees planning the outdoor course incorporated all kinds of nature-provided challenges including rose bushes, tree roots, battering winds and dense brush.

Much of the hive stayed close to home today, eager to watch the event unfold. The whole place was lively and full of excitement. Near the podium, the hive leaders began convening to judge the indoor agility course. Courage, Sting, Royal, Nectar, and Sugar seated themselves in a row. Several respected hive members had been recruited to watch the competition closely from various angles, and one bee had a dandelion petal and birch paper booklet ready to record their findings and determine scores. As the minutes ticked by, the hive members began organizing themselves into seated rows wherever they could find room, and the competitors came into view.

Crystal was participant #1. Her demeanor was quite captivating. She was solid as a rock and as confident as a newborn could be. She was eyeing her competition discreetly, and could be seen stretching or flexing in preparation for the race. She was clearly competitive. Next to her stood participant #2, Amethyst. She almost didn't seem present. Her expression was wistful and airy, as if her head were up in the clouds. The young queen glided about now and then to glance into the crowd of bees, as if searching for something.

Blossom, #3, was a ball of nerves. Her demeanor was rigid and shivering, and her eyes looked wild and panicked. She paced nervously, studying each part of the agility test to gauge them. She passed by the other competitors various times, almost oblivious to her nearest surroundings. #4, called Amber, stood looking thoughtful. She looked at the course, then the crowd. She often turned her head to the hive leaders, observing each of them with curiosity. She seemed a little nervous, but not overly so.

It was time for the Games to begin. Queen Royal stood at the podium, gesturing for the crowd's attention. After several moments, the room settled into a near silence and she began. "It is time for the Queen Games to commence!" Everyone clapped and cheered. "Our first game will be a thrilling, close-quartered, indoor agility race. Our competitors will not be allowed to fly at any time during this course. They will each race individually. Their speed will be a large part of their final scores, but other things taken into account will include grace, ease of execution, and lack of course disturbance. Each misplaced obstacle will dock points. Now remember, this competition is mostly for fun and entertainment. Enjoy!"

The spectators cheered in excitement, as they passed Royal's explanations to every corner of the large room. The four young queens were lined up. It seemed that for this competition, they would go in order of their numbers. Crystal, then, was first in line and ready to go.

The bright and capable young queen was thrilling to watch. She maneuvered the course with a speed and grace unmatched. She didn't miss any obstacle, nor did she bump anything to dock points. Her run flew by, and was flawless. The crowd cheered with excitement and wonder at her accomplishment. There was a lull as the scorekeeper made hurried notes. The scores would not be revealed until the end, but it was clear that #1 would be hard to beat.

Next, Amethyst was up. She seemed as though she'd just awakened from a dream as the course lay right ahead of her. Taken a bit off guard, she stumbled ahead. It seemed like each obstacle surprised her, since she hadn't taken much notice of them before. She was not prepared. She couldn't help but stumble, and a few of the obstacles fell down as she attempted them. This, of course, docked points. Her performance was many marks below Crystal's, to be sure.

After her run, the crowd let out some pitying sounds. A crew came to reassemble the course for competitor #3. After all was set, Blossom was up. She was rigid with concern, eyeing the course woefully. Crystal nudged her in, a bit impatient, and the nervous queen's time started. She clearly overthought every step she took. In doing so, she avoided most blunders. But her run was slow and tedious, and she didn't flow gracefully. By the end, she had bumped one obstacle, and taken twice as long as competitor #1.

The crowd clapped tentatively, eager to watch another competitive run. After the course was restored, it was Amber's turn. She took a breath and launched herself onto the course. She operated with a graceful stride, and her speed was competitive. The crowd got excited, and cheers erupted in support. As she stumbled and tripped on an obstacle, the crowd let out exclamations of distress, but she recovered well and finished the rest of the race without another mistake. The bright young queen let out an accomplished gasp, her face showing a modest mixture of accomplishment and apprehension.

The crowd's attention turned to the record keeper expectantly. After several minutes, she reported to the Queen. Royal stood to announce the placings, and the hive buzzed with excitement.

"For the indoor agility course, your final placings are as follows. In fourth place, we have Amethyst, competitor #2! In third, competitor

#3, Blossom!" Royal allotted a pause for excitement to grow in the crowd. "Second place is Amber and first place is Crystal! Our winner is Crystal, #1!" Each spectator cheered in excitement for several seconds, and the four queens reacted to hearing their placements. Blossom looked disappointed, and Crystal looked mighty proud.

"In an hour, the outdoor race will begin! The queens will be made familiar with the track and given some time to rest. Please return after a brief intermission." The hive dispersed, briefly attending to various day-to-day tasks as they waited.

The hive leaders turned to one another to discuss things in more detail. Courage spoke first. "Crystal certainly has talent and grace. But I'm curious to see if she becomes overly confident."

"Yes, true." Royal responded. "Still, she is a promising contender."

"I like Amethyst." Nectar smiled. "Though I'm not sure if her personality is ideal for a queen, she certainly doesn't care what anyone thinks of her."

"She's a bit of an airhead!" Sugar couldn't help but offer.

Sting chuckled. "She's a bit detached at this stage. We'll have to see if she remains that way. Now Blossom was riddled with anxiety from start to finish during this race. Her run wasn't a disaster, but I hope her nerves will quiet down. Otherwise, they'll rob her of any chance to win the title."

Royal buzzed. "I really liked Amber's run. She doesn't lack grace or skill, and she maintained a very balanced countenance that I found notable." The other leaders nodded in agreement.

The hour moved fast, as the event coordinators and young queens were kept pretty busy. It felt like no time at all before the outdoor course was set to begin. Much of the hive had found seats in trees and bushes along the course. The four queens were lined up at the starting line, and for this race, they'd compete all at once.

The four queens waited together in anticipation.

"Ughh, I don't remember if the tree roots come second or third!" Blossom couldn't keep still as she flew back and forth anxiously.

"I think they come third," Amber offered, "after navigating through the rosebush!"

"Oh thank you! Wait, are you trying to trick me?"

Amber looked shocked. "Oh no!" But Blossom still eyed her suspiciously.

Crystal chuckled. "You need to pay closer attention. They ran us through the course twice, and it's not overly complicated." She stretched her wings. "I'm ready to fly like the wind!"

Amber glanced toward Amethyst curiously. The young queen seemed totally unconcerned about their next competition. "What is it that occupies your mind, Amethyst?" She asked.

"Huh? Oh. I'm just seeing who I can see. You never know, my love might be watching right now. Oh, I can't wait to meet him!" She twirled in flight wistfully.

"Oh!" Amber smiled. "Well I'm sure he'd be mighty impressed if you win this race."

Amethyst's eyes sparked with realization. "You're right! Can... can you remind me what the order of events is? I seem to have forgotten!" The hopeless romantic seemed armed with a new purpose and vigor. Amber obliged.

Crystal eyed Amber skeptically. "Odd strategy, queen. Bolstering your competition."

Amber looked thoughtful. "Well, I want to really earn this win. The more competition, the merrier!"

Crystal laughed. "You are a strange one, Amber. Oh! Look alive, we start in a moment!"

The queens focused their attention outward, and the nerves were building. It was a thrill to compete in this way, and the whole hive was cheering them on. An announcement was made, and the seconds ticked away in uncomfortable silence. 3, 2, 1, GO!

The four queens took off with equal steam. The wind battered against them at the start of the race, and they struggled against its power. The first obstacle was to weave between two great branches of a tall oak. Excited spectators cheered as the four queens ascended upward toward them. At this point in the race, they were fairly neck and neck. Currently in the lead, Amethyst pushed on with surprising prowess. Crystal huffed in frustration not far behind.

After passing through the branches, they were to turn left and descend toward a thick and perilous rosebush. They could only go in single file, and the pace was slow. Bees all around cheered as they entered and exited its thorny grasp. They continued with great speed toward the low tangled roots ahead. Crystal had taken the lead, and appeared increasingly confident. But as she passed through the root, she went too fast and snagged a wing in flight. It was enough to cause her to falter and lose her lead.

Amber hesitated on the other side of the roots, looking back to ensure that Crystal was okay. The queen recovered and rejoined the race, falling into fourth place. Amethyst maintained the lead with the anxious Blossom coming in near second. There were a couple other turns and obstacles, but the placement remained the same. With exclamations of surprise and excitement, the four queens passed the finish line in that order. Amethyst, Blossom, Amber, and Crystal.

An announcer proclaimed the placing loudly for all to hear, and everybee cheered. Crystal was fuming at the finish line. "No! No, if it weren't for my stupid misjudgement, I would've won this easily!" She was not happy.

"Are you okay?" Amber asked, eyeing Crystal's disheveled wing.

"Of course I'm okay. I mean, no! I'm not. What's with rousing our competition? Amethyst would never have been a threat if it weren't for you!" Crystal huffed, turning away.

Blossom was looking a bit at ease. "I'm proud of my second!"

"You seemed to relax a bit this time! It served you well!" Amber encouraged her. The young queen swelled with the affirmation.

Amethyst was busy scanning the crowd, seeing who may be admiring her valiant win. She was on cloud nine, again living in her own world.

At that, the events of the day came to an end, and the exhausted queens and spectators turned in for a good sleep. They needed to rest before another big day tomorrow.

Chapter 8: The Winning Queen

The following days were filled with more tests and competitions. Day 2 had been focused around mental sharpness, decision making, and strategy. Placements varied quite a bit, but Amethyst consistently scored lower that day. Often, her answers seemed misguided, and her priorities were certainly unique. Crystal had taken the lead overall. She was certainly sharp, and she knew it. No bee could deny that she'd be a formidable leader. Amber had shown promise too. Her decisions were balanced with both empathy and logic, which appealed to many. As for Blossom, she seemed a bit jumpy, leading her to more knee-jerk reactions that may not yield the best outcomes.

It was the final day, and the focus was wisdom and faith. The tests involved various verbal questions in which morality, integrity, and competence were necessary. Today, Crystal and Amber had been neck and neck. As the day went on, Amber pulled into the lead. She really shined in these areas, and persisted even as other competitors became mentally drained.

Throughout the three-day ordeal, each of the four queens had garnered fans. There were special aspects to each of them, and various drones were eager to impress one of the she-bees. Some hive mates were excited about the possibility of branching off and establishing new hives with the queens who didn't replace Royal.

The hive leaders had taken many things into account as they observed the games. Royal probably had the most influential say in the end, and she had paid special attention to how each competitor handled adversity. She was looking for someone who could take on the load she bore. No bee here other than herself knew just how heavy it felt at times.

Sugar tried to decide whom she could get along with for the rest of her life. She had her own reservations about each queen, and her own strong opinions. But a certain favorite had definitely risen in her mind, based on her observations and notions. Nectar seemed to agree with her, but was never totally forthcoming about her own thoughts. She stayed a bit mysterious as usual. It seemed only Royal knew what Nectar was really thinking at all times.

Courage had watched for someone with strong moral integrity and promising faith. He knew how important a queen like that would be in this next stage of hive life. Sting added a perspective of strength and resolve. He felt it necessary that the next queen could bear heavy loads and manage many things. He knew all about the organizational skills required to run the hive each day.

It was time for the hive vote. Throughout the evening, and after the final games concluded, bees submitted their ballots until sundown. The record keeper and hive leadership convened, discussing thoroughly until the count came in. After weighing every score and opinion, hive leadership made their decision, and it was time for the grand reveal.

The four queens stood near the podium, full of nerves. Nearly the entire hive squeezed themselves into the landing grounds, anxious to hear the results. After everybee was ready, Royal stood to present the facts.

"Thank you all for participating in this exciting ordeal. I am proud of all four competitors, and each will make an excellent queen. I'd like to start by presenting the competition results and the popular vote. These may or may not reflect our final decision. At the very end, I will announce which bee we have chosen to be the next Queen of Hive Honey Quest."

The room rippled with excitement as Royal continued. "Results from each category of tests varied greatly! We saw first-hand how multi-talented and diverse our girls are. After day one, a clear leader was not determined. Placements varied so widely! Crystal won a race and Amethyst another. Amber and Blossom ranked secondary. All four queens were determined to be fully developed, fine mothers-to-be. On day two, Crystal began to take the lead. Her sharp mental acuity was notable. Then, today, Amber rose to recognition in her emotional intelligence and wisdom. Overall, each queen has proven that they can lead a hive."

Royal took a breath as the hive waited. "You all have entered your votes, and the bee winning the popular vote is... Crystal!" Cheers erupted in the room. Crystal had definitely captivated many of them. As the noise died down, Royal continued. "After carefully considering every result, the popular vote, and taking into account our understanding of the job at hand, we have settled on a winner. We have chosen our next queen. The queen to be my successor is... Amber!"

The crowd went wild. Amber had been second in the popular vote, and they didn't have a dispute with the winner. Crystal stood, completely shocked. She looked blankly at Amber, defeated. Blossom seemed almost relieved, and Amethyst didn't seem to care much at all.

"We will now have a short acceptance speech from the winning queen!" Royal gestured to Amber welcomingly.

Amber approached the podium slowly. "Wow, I'm... shocked and honored. I promise I will do my best to fill this role well and serve the hive for as long as I live." She stepped away, too overcome with amazement to say more.

"There will be a crowning ceremony in due time, after a little bit of training. The other queens will be given a few days to make arrangements before leaving the hive. Whether they want to strategize their hive placements, recruit workers, or find love, they have three days to do whatever is needed. They will have the opportunity to begin their own legacies and write their own stories. Thank you all for participating, and have a good night!"

After the great announcement, there were plans for a party. The landing grounds were quickly cleared, tidied up, and made into a great banquet. The four queens were to attend, and any bee who wanted to meet them would partake. A great and plentiful feast was to be served. As the arrangements unfolded, it was pretty late into the night before the event actually began. The four queens had assumed their own corners of the room, and admirers for each collected where they wished. Amber's corner was plumb full, as well as Crystal's. Blossom and Amethyst had a sizable crowd as well, and all four had many hopeful suitors approaching them.

Amber was an excellent choice for queen. Her personality and attitude much resembled Royal's younger self. She was full of compassion and care, while also being capable both mentally and physically. She sat at her table, overwhelmed by the crowd gathering before her. *Wow... I can't believe it!* She was definitely excited about her win, but also, a great sense of responsibility weighed on her. *I need to do a good job here.* She looked forward to learning as much as she could from Royal.

The meal came first, and sitting with her at their exclusive table was Sugar. The nurse bee-in-training had not spoken just yet, as the room was loud and she was clearly nervous. Finally, she turned to the young queen to strike up a conversation.

"Well, how does it feel to be the chosen one?"

Amber smiled weakly. "It feels good, but it's a lot of responsibility. I want to do a good job. Right now, I pretty much know nothing. Training under Royal will definitely help."

Sugar seemed to like her answer. "You definitely seem up for the task."

"How long have you been training?" Amber asked politely.

"A couple weeks now, I think." Sugar buzzed. "I really like it so far. Nectar is fascinating and wise."

"She sure seems that way!" Amber smiled widely. "I suppose you and I are going to be close comrades."

"Yeah. Hopefully we get along." Sugar winked. "So far, so good."

The two began their feast. It was grand indeed. There were various fresh flowers plucked right before sundown. Several mixtures of nectar, honey, and pollen were offered. Some were delicacies. The meal didn't seem very lengthy, and it was not long before bees made their way to the queen's tables to meet them.

A strapping young drone approached Amber with confidence. He was handsome, for sure, but he came off quite strong. He seemed confident that his introduction would leave a lasting impression as he strode away. Many other drones came forward. Some shy, some confident. Some young, some older, some accomplished and some generally untalented. Sugar appeared to have appreciated one or two, but not a drone succeeded in standing out to Amber. *Hm, I'm not too sure about these drones.*

Until he came forward. At first glance, she noticed something different about him. She couldn't identify quite what, but it was striking. The ruddy lad was mature but not old, and his eyes glittered with a sort of spark. He looked like he had a passion for life. When he approached her table, he pulled a chair and sat in front of her rather than stooping down to shake her hand. "Hi Amber! My name is Justice. It's great to meet you." His dazzling smile graced her, and she couldn't help but get shy.

"Oh, um... It's great to meet you, Justice!" She was surprised by her own lack of words in front of this drone. Just his presence made her a good kind of nervous. Sugar seemed to catch on, and filled the silence.

"You know, no drone has claimed her first dance yet. I think you might have a good shot!" She winked.

The drone smiled, amused. "I'd like that! When does the dance start?"

"I think it starts soon." Amber mustered the words. Her face was red from Sugar's suggestion, though secretly she was grateful. The fascinating drone looked at her warmly.

"Is it alright if I sit with you two until it starts?"

"Of course!" Sugar answered, and the minutes passed agonizingly slow as they fumbled through some more introductory conversation.

The event passed on into the wee hours of the night, and each queen made important connections with possible mates and workers who may attend their departures. Over the next three days, these connections grew stronger and decisions were made.

For Crystal, the plan was to head southeast, deeper into Shadow Forest, to find an ideal place to build several miles away. She had garnered a crowd of about fifty devoted workers, and had selected a brawny drone called Purpose for a mate. She had everything well organized and figured out.

Amethyst, despite her constant searching, hadn't found the perfect mate. Blossom was also struggling to establish such a connection. So, the two decided to find a drone congregation area together and cement the rest of their plans later. A few workers, maybe ten in total, had decided to attend the queens in hopes of helping one of them build their new hives. They also could help protect the queens along the way.

Amber had begun training under Royal, and continued her courtship of the witty drone Justice. Being careful and intentional about all of her decisions, she was not in a rush to seal the deal. She knew that whichever mate she chose would become the next King. That was no small consideration. And so, the three days of preparations passed.

Chapter 9: Queen Quests

The two young queens called Amethyst and Blossom were optimistic as they and their ten or so workers departed from Hive Honey Quest. They were heading north and a little west to the closest known congregation area, which happened to be somewhat near the wild hive's forest edge. Amethyst exuded a blissful giddiness while Blossom appeared shy but hopeful. They pressed on with intention, knowing that as queens, their time outside of a hive should be extremely rare. They needed to start building their new lives as soon as possible if they hoped to survive.

It was a warm, inviting day and Flowerbud was turning into Flowerbloom. The breeze bumped them gently at their backs as they flew along, accelerating their pace. It was only minutes before the usual congregation area was in sight.

"Oh, I'm so excited!" Amethyst's eyes were starry. "I think the one who will love me is there. I can feel it!" She twirled mid-air in pre-celebration.

Blossom let out a short, nervous sigh. "I don't know, sister. I'm pretty sure my wings are gonna freeze up and I'll plummet to the ground." She shuddered. "This is so scary! All those strangers!"

"You mean exciting!" Amethyst spun around. "Come on, Blossom! You're gorgeous, and they'd be a fool not to like you. Now let's go!"

The workers trailed not far behind, getting ready to settle a small distance away from the meeting place. Their queens would enter alone. With a little encouragement, Amethyst nudged Blossom forward and the two made their grand entrance.

There was a small crowd of drones who had likely spent hours waiting in this place. It was a wide open section of the field, abloom with especially bright and beautiful flowers. The setting was a particularly romantic place. Drones of every variation perked up with fervent interest at their arrival. They were all extremely eager to have a word with the newcomers.

"Hey ladies!" "Come over here!" "How are you?" "Look this way!"

Amethyst almost melted from the attention, while Blossom was scared right into her shell and eager to leave immediately. Amethyst made sure she stayed though. The queens flew casually about, taking in each contender and chatting to themselves. Some drones were built and handsome. Others were average sized with a wholesome face. Some were oddly proportioned and even ugly, and the attitudes of all varied a lot. Overall, most of the drones were extremely eager and desperate. In addition to this, almost none reminded the queens of the drones at home, who tended to be larger and stronger than average.

Just then, a large and powerful drone came into sight. Amethyst squealed and approached him directly. His countenance was respectful and gentlemanly, and yet his presence commanded the attention of those around him. Drones looked upon him dejectedly, sure that their chances had been squelched.

"Hello there sir..." Amethyst made a shy smile as she greeted the tall stranger. He looked at her, his eyes full of tamed interest and warmth.

"Hi there! The name is Ash. It's nice to meet you two." He bowed in a practiced and grandiose manner before the two maidens. The drone showed just the right amount of interest and respect to really draw them in.

"He's mine." Amethyst nudged Blossom quietly, who had no problem with that. She began to slink away when the drone called out.

"Wait! Don't go, dear. I have a friend or two you may like to meet. They are gentle and kind."

The timid queen hesitated before deciding to stay. The drone proceeded to ask them friendly questions which made for very enjoyable conversations. He had a way about him. Everything he said was perfect and captivating, and it wasn't long before the queens had decided for sure to stay near him. The other drones in the congregation area didn't try to intervene. The large drone's stature and presence was intimidating to them, and they figured they should stay out of it altogether and wait for other queens.

Maybe an hour had passed and the sun had traveled a bit in the sky. Ash looked up. "Wow, time flies when I'm talking with you!" He directed his comment to Amethyst, who by now, was completely sold. She stared up at him with strong infatuation as he spoke. "Why don't we ditch this crowd. I can bring you to where I'm staying, and maybe a friend or two of mine would have a chance at catching your eye." He smiled at Blossom invitingly.

The queens mutually agreed, and went to fetch their small entourage. In no time at all, they and the ten workers were following Ash toward the Edge of Ally Forest where the wild hive dwelled.

"Oh, are you from the Hive of Soldiers?" Amethyst gasped in approval. "What an honorable drone you must be!"

The drone smiled. "Maybe, wait and see my dear."

They all flew in silent anticipation. After flying into the forest about a mile, Ash slowed to a stop. They were surrounded closely by small brush, and they couldn't see far in any direction. Confused, Amethyst buzzed.

"Where exactly are you staying?"

"Oh, we are about halfway there. I just figured you would like to rest your wings for a moment." He gestured welcomingly to a small branch which he had found his seat on. "Come, sit with me."

Amethyst blushed and joined him shyly, while Blossom and the workers sat nearby. After maybe five minutes of rest and chatting, they heard an explosive sound. Scores of previously concealed drones began shouting, pouring from their hiding places to completely surround the lot. The queens shrieked in fear and surprise as they and each of their attending entourage were roughly seized by strong arms. No matter how hard they fought, they couldn't escape.

Amethyst looked wildly to Ash, her eyes pleading for help. Much to her dismay, the drone's expression changed to one of pride and accomplishment. He smiled broadly and laughed. "Do you think one of these drones might suit your friend?" Amethyst's face changed to one of rage.

"How could you! I... I loved you!" She tore at her captor with vicious anger while the large drone continued laughing.

"Don't worry my dears. All will be well! You have found yourselves a forever home." The drone turned to the others to give some instructions, and the swarm took off to continue heading north.

Buzzz led the group proudly. *Yes, I've done it! At last I will be able to build my army to its completion. At last I will settle my debts to our allies. It's almost time for vengeance... and the restoration of my reign in Hive Honey Quest!*

COURAGE SIGHED. IT had been a long, busy day. Between general mentorship and New Beginning rehabilitations, he had not gotten much rest for months. Thankfully, a couple new mentors had been chosen recently to help share the load. But ever since, huge changes and events in the hive had kept him scrambling.

Since the attack on Royal from New Beginning and the fall thereafter, Courage had been fully endorsed as a member of the hive's leadership. Weighty tasks and projects continued to wisen and age the drone beyond his years. He often advised Royal as closely as Nectar did, and he'd become close to King Sting as well. It was said that Courage's presence would ease the transition as a new queen and nurse bee were instated.

A few weeks had now passed since the Queen Games. Amber was ready for crowning, and Sugar, likewise, was now fit to join at her side. Training had been a prevalent focus for so long, but at last the hive was ready for change. Royal had made her intention known that the transfer of power would occur any day now.

With all of this and more weighing heavily on his mind, Courage sat in his cell. His sister had said she would come visit tonight and he figured she'd show up any moment now. As he waited, he tried to relax his busy mind and shift into a more relaxed state. *Meadow.* No matter how hard he tried, she was the most present thought in his brain. He only saw her once in a while, and it had been a long time. Most of the times he met with someone in his dreams recently, it was Forest. That drone had proved to be an excellent and valuable friend to him as he navigated his strange life. But still, his heart always longed for his mate. *One day. We will be reunited as soon as my work here is done.* Courage smiled and closed his eyes as he pictured her delicate and beautiful face.

It was then that Joy knocked at his door, and he reluctantly cleared his mind and stood up. He opened the door to greet his beloved sister. "Joy! Great to see you! How are you?"

She trotted in like she'd had the best day of her life. "Hi brother!" She plopped herself onto his cushion without restraint. "I'm great! How are you?"

"Very good! Just tired. Tell me more about your day."

Joy lit up. "Oh, training has been so incredible. And now, I am one of the most learned Enemy Researchers from my group. I get to teach the new bees! You would be amazed at how much information there is in this brain." She pointed at her head humorously. "It's crazy!"

Courage smiled. Joy was naturally passionate and bubbly, but ever since she'd found her niche, it had been off the charts. Her excitement about the subject she studied made her quickly excel. She was always eager to learn more. "You sure shine in this area, Joy!"

Joy smiled radiantly. Then, she paused, glancing around conspiratorially. "You'll never guess what I saw today on my excursion."

"What?" Courage cocked his head, interested.

"I saw yellowjackets." She shuddered a bit. "Of course I stayed far away, but there were more than I've ever seen around here at one time. I reported it to my superior just before coming here."

"Where?" Courage asked, suddenly troubled.

"Nearby! They were right at the edge of our forest, probably twenty or more of them. It's normal to see one here and there, but a group like that could indicate that they're seeking a place to build a home. Still, it's quite late in the season for yellowjackets to establish a new hive..." She rubbed her chin curiously. "It was odd enough to report, for sure."

"Hmm." This information was striking Courage more than he would expect. *Something about this isn't good.* "Well, hopefully it's nothing!" He forced a smile for his sister. She looked at him for a long time.

"You're a strange one, you know?" She bumped him playfully. "Sometimes it seems like there's a whole world going on inside your head that no one else is a part of." She laughed.

"Oh really?" Courage batted back at her, forcing a chuckle. *Ugh, she's onto me.* He had always felt that his private story should stay just that - private. He hadn't shared anything about his past life or unique situation with anyone. Not Royal, not Nectar, not Joy. The Queen and her nurse bee had always seemed aware in some strange way that he was special, but they didn't pry. With Joy, it was different. She was painfully curious, and it was actually very hard for Courage to keep such massive secrets from her. She often inquired about his special someone, but she didn't know that this someone was spiritual rather than physical. Courage often felt lonely in keeping these things secret, but he knew that sharing it could have its own myriad of consequences as well.

"You're doing it again!" Joy peered at him. "You know, I say pretty much everything I think, and you seem to say maybe ten percent."

"You might be right about that." Courage smiled weakly. "I do a lot of internal processing, I guess."

Changing the subject, Joy buzzed curiously. "Have you seen Meadow lately? Surely it's time to go be with her once and for all. Our lives are only so long you know." She winked.

"I think the time is soon, but not yet. I have lots to do here first, especially since becoming a part of our hive leadership. I need to oversee the transition of the crown, and I should finish my work as much as possible with rehabilitation."

Joy looked at him, concerned. "I think if you stay too long, you will never escape the pressures of your position. You may never get to be with her. I don't want to be a bad influence, but I just hope that your own happiness doesn't have to be last on your list of goals."

Courage let out a sigh. He couldn't tell her that his love was far away, and that his life here was only a drop in the eternity he would spend by her side. He himself often wondered when he'd be able to go home. It wasn't easy to be here, where pain and toil and hardship were a part of everyday life. Sighing again, he looked at Joy soberly. "I wish I could share all of my thoughts with you, but there are too many to count. Just know this... I *will* accomplish my task here in this hive, and then I will be with her. Forever. And I'll be sure to visit you as often as I can when that time comes. My life isn't necessarily simple, and it can be very hard at times. But I know I am doing what I need to be doing." He smiled at Joy. "And I'm very lucky to have a sister like you who cares for me so much."

Joy seemed satisfied by this answer, and she rested her head on his shoulder. "I love you Courage! And you bless me just as much."

Chapter 10: A New Era

Now, as speedily as ever, the time had come to transition to new leadership. As many bees as could fit in the landing grounds stood to witness the passing of titles to the new leaders, and they each delivered a speech.

"I now pass on my title as Queen of Hive Honey Quest to you, Amber. May Lighthive guide you, and enable you to be the best Queen you can be. May you exude grace and lead with wisdom, drawing strength also from those around you."

"And I now pass on my title as King of Hive Honey Quest to you, Justice. May Lighthive give you strength as you stand beside your Queen. May you lead the troops with pride, protect your home, and carry the torch to the next generations."

"And I now pass on my title as nurse bee to you, Sugar. You will advise Queen Amber and King Justice as they take this new path. May the Light you have harbored within pour out upon the hive leadership, keeping their steps straight and their pursuits pure."

The hive erupted into excited, deafening cheers as the three new hive leaders bowed before them. Royal, Sting, and Nectar stood behind them, clapping and tearful. The two she-bees were showing clear signs of age, and the whole hive knew their time was coming to pass on. Sting would likely live on for quite some time, robbed of his soulmate. This was a time of both celebration and sadness, as the love everybee had for them would not cease. It would take time to adjust to the new leaders. They would be unique and different, and there'd be a learning curve as they began their reign. In some ways, the hive would be vulnerable for a while until everything really settled and clicked.

The crowning ceremony had been long and tedious. Royal had given a lengthy speech, expressing her deep love and gratitude for every hive member. She reminded them of all they had been through, from her arrival until now. They had lived under a time of harsh, tyrannical rule. Then, they navigated through internal struggles as each bee tried to find their place. The New Beginning cult had enslaved many minds, but now, even some of the most hopeless ex-members were finding their footing again. Hive Honey Quest had grown from being a place where faith could never be discussed, into a place where the majority of bees found peace and purpose in the Light. They had the free will to choose what they believed, and leaders were just. Time had truly mended many deep wounds, and Royal encouraged them that a season of peace and harmony lay not far ahead. Many tears were shed as she'd reflected on the hive's history.

The ceremony was followed by celebrations. There were beedances held, leading workers to some of the most delicious and beautiful flowers of Flowerbloom. Amber and Justice took a flight together and the hive cheered to send them off. Royal and Sting also meandered outside, no longer bound by the extreme protection an active queen lived under. The two nurse bees, young and old, sat together simply watching the hive celebrations and occasionally exchanging meaningful words.

What a time of transition. Not only was the hive brimming with newness and vibrant life, but it was distracted and a bit disorganized. So much had occurred in such a short time. Over the next weeks, they only just began to adapt to these changes. And even though things were different now, many bees were finding their footing. Mentorship, comradery, purpose, and faith began to grow a tender stability within the hearts of everybee. The hive began to have a taste of what peace lay ahead, and were slowly growing into a strong and unified force. Finally, after months of turmoil and challenge, there was true deliverance from past bondage occurring. Hive Honey Quest was stronger than it had been in so long.

But nothing could prepare them for the final fight that lurked right around the corner.

BUZZZ'S EYES GLEAMED with victory as he gazed at the small crowd of newborns before him. *At last.* He had been able to settle his debts with the allies, all while finally starting to build his own ranks once again.

The two queens he had captured a few weeks ago had been put to good use. Blossom was given to the allies as promised to begin a honey bee brood for their own use, and Amethyst became Buzzz's queen. She was already producing thousands of eggs, and the first pupae had just emerged. These bees were strong and pleasing to Buzzz, mirroring many of his traits. He had been quite lucky to acquire a queen from Hive Honey Quest, where strong genes were prevalent as well. *Nothing but the best for me and my army.*

"Newborns! Welcome to your family." Buzzz had a special skill for charisma and control as a leader, and he was confident these bees would require very little training. "Stand proud! You serve a hive that is a mark above the rest. You will play a key role in our domination of those who have wronged us. You will help us restore justice. Are you strong enough?" He paced in front of them with both confidence and authority. "You must be. There is no other choice but death. Prove to me your ability, and undying loyalty, and you will be rewarded." He grinned at them, firing them up. Whoops and cheers filled the room. "In only a few short days, we will settle the scores. Rise! Show me your worth!"

After this speech, Buzzz left the newborns to their trainers. It was important that he was a god in their eyes. He wouldn't be the one inflicting discomfort, but the one they had faith in. He was the one they would go through anything for. Buzzz had practiced his role well. He'd learned from his past blunders, though they were of course few.

There was no room for defeat this time around, and he knew for a fact that his army would prevail. *No one will be able to withstand us. One glance at our allies and everybee will be scrambling and surrendered. But if not, of course, we fight. Our numbers will be unmatched. They stand no chance.*

Buzzz soaked in that bubbling rage deep within. He had been wronged, disrespected! He would never allow that to happen again. He would never allow those who tried to defile him to live in peace.

He approached his office, and made his way to the queen cell in the corner where Amethyst stayed. For the first week, the queen had cried pitifully without end. She was absolutely exhausting and aggravating. Still, Buzzz was being far-sighted about this. Instead of crushing her without concern, he knew his coming years would be a lot easier if she loved and respected him. That way he could sleep in peace at night and grow his following without an obstacle.

He spent the last two weeks building her trust in him, and she proved an ideal pupil. Her affections were quite easily earned. While she wasn't as doting of him as when they had first met, she was more and more devoted to him each day. He gave her just enough to keep her under his secret control. He said sweet things to her and let her believe that he loved her. Even though he was the one to originally capture her, Buzzz had used his mastery of deception to bring her back to his service. He spun a beautiful and convincing web of lies and was very good at maintaining it. Somehow, he had even explained away his role in her capture. Her eyes now lit up whenever he graced her with his presence. *I've got her now.*

"Amethyst! Our children are perfect." He smiled at her with fabricated affection. "You were made to be a mother."

The young queen swelled under his praise. "Oh but Buzzz, when can we move into a real home? This place is becoming cramped, and we are only just beginning to grow our legacy!"

"Only a few days now, dear. In a few days, we will take what is rightfully ours."

Amethyst's brow furrowed slightly. Buzzz had recognized the necessity of telling her that Hive Honey Quest was his target. He knew that she wouldn't respond well to storming her previous home if he didn't prime her mind first. He still had a little bit of work to do though, as she remained slightly resistant to the idea. She forced a weak smile. "Oh, isn't there a much grander home that we can build ourselves? I have lots of ideas for designs..."

"No!" Buzzz raised his voice the perfect amount, then lowered it. He knew how to assert his authority over a queen with tact. "There is no other option, dear. I've been through this with you several times. Remember, the hive is my home. It was taken from me. I will not allow them to maintain victory over me. Instead, I will bring justice! We will have a real hive - *our* real hive, very soon." He searched her eyes with intention, sighing with satisfaction as he saw them soften just a little more.

"Yeah. They shouldn't have done that to you."

Buzzz moved toward her to give her a touch of affection. He always knew to make a habit of rewarding good behavior in the beginning. It was all part of keeping control over a queen. He also punished poor behavior, using tactics such as dominance, ignoring, and withholding. The first months of such relationships were key. After some time, it was quite low maintenance to keep the upper hand, and Buzzz had been lucky to find such an easy victim to control. Amethyst already required very little to remain warm toward him - almost bread crumbs.

"Of course, you will stay here until we've won the battle. You must stay safe." Buzzz let her believe his concern was coming from love, when in reality it was all about his needs for life going forward. "Then, we will come back for you and escort you to safety."

Amethyst's eyes looked dreamy. "Oh, what a life we'll have! When we have more space, everything will be better."

"Yes dear." Buzzz patted her head before leaving her chamber. She looked longingly after him. "Won't you... stay?"

Buzzz hesitated. *Hmm, is it time to make my presence more of a luxury? Or is it time to give her just a little more assurance?* He only paused for a moment before responding. "I can't, dear. I am a very busy drone. Please, let me have some peace." And with that, he turned away from her dejected form without care. *Yes. That was exactly what is needed right now. She must know that she is a burden.* Buzzz took a moment to appreciate his own tact before retiring to his desk to mull over plans.

In just three days, his months of brooding would come to a head. He would arrive with powerful weapons and be unstoppable. But Buzzz spent more time thinking about how to handle surprises this time. While it was against his nature to be realistic about any of his own shortcomings, deep down he knew he wouldn't be making a fool of himself again by underestimating his enemy. Buzzz had to somewhat acknowledge that he'd been over optimistic in the past, which led to dire consequences. He could see this only a little, and never dared to voice it or dwell on it. Instead he directed the subtle awareness toward greater plans and efforts. If asked, he would still adamantly deny any personal flaws.

Buzzz's mind raced with battle strategies and training schedules. He spent many hours into the night obsessing over them, unable to rest. Finally, a couple hours before sunrise, he fell asleep on his desk. Still, his weary, haunted mind raced with unpleasant dreams.

Chapter 11: Darkness

Buzzz had gone to every effort to strengthen his army. This wasn't just limited to physical preparations and manipulation. He had also intentionally sought dark spiritual aid.

For most of his life, Buzzz had nurtured a powerful hate toward Lighthive and anything to do with such faith. And for a while, he abandoned all things spiritual, whether good or bad. But after narrowly escaping the War of the Ghost with his life, he had found himself in a place of desperation. He was willing to consider almost anything in order to regain power and strength.

It was then that he began convening with darkness. Similar to the Honeycrystal, there were certain ways to contact and communicate with Darkhive. Buzzz had discovered one, and began building a rapport. It was by the dark beings' suggestion that he formed his current alliance, and by their guidance that he honed his skills as a formidable leader. He now had even more power over the minds of his followers than ever before.

Unfortunately, Darkhive never worked for free. The more he visited with them, the more they took control over him. He didn't know this of course, but he was losing sovereignty of his own self. Darkness had him in chains and ready to do its command. As time went on, Buzzz was expected to meet with them more often, and they even began to torment him day and night. He wasn't able to rest without fear.

Of course Buzzz was in denial about this "hindrance". No one ever saw him weak, and neither did he allow himself to recognize how truly controlled he was. How afraid. A deep feeling of dread hunted him whenever his tired mind tried to slow down. Because of this, he made a subconscious point to always stay busy. This race was wearing him down. He told himself he was stronger than ever when in reality he was closest to breaking.

Even as he slept, darkness crept into his dreams. He saw shadows lurking, chasing him down. He saw a black night, void of the light from the moon or stars. But worse than what he saw was what he felt: a horrible emptiness within... desolation, and constant fear. Stirring restlessly, he forced his eyes open. Buzzz blinked to fix his bleary vision and shook his fur. He stood up quickly as his stiff joints groaned. Exhaustion tore at him, causing his head to pound. He had managed to get a couple hours of sleep, but there was no more rest for him. It was time to start the day.

It seemed that as the ambush grew near, his torment grew worse, but Buzzz shoved it down like always. He knew this battle would award him true victory. He figured that then, he would rest quite well.

And so, Buzzz proceeded in his preparations until the day he planned to attack.

HIVE HONEY QUEST WAS quite peaceful. Most bees had settled into a pleasing routine, from play fighting and beedances to delicious pollination. Their walls were down. Well, for everyone but Sugar.

The young nurse bee couldn't ignore the pressure she felt that something was about to happen. She sat at Nectar's side as she slept - the little nurse bee had been declining for days. *Ugh, how can I do this without you?* She studied her mentor's face. Upon it rested an expression of pure peace and bliss. Sugar knew Nectar's moments were few remaining. She sadly watched the slow, steady breath rise and fall from her mentor's lungs, aware that any inhale might be her last.

Something is coming. Something is at our doorstep.

Sugar clenched her jaw with frustration. *But I want to be at her side when she goes!* Sugar knew that her duty took precedence over that desire, but she voiced it all the same. It seemed that Lighthive could handle her emotions. Regretfully, she willed her body to stand. She looked down with sad affection at Nectar, the wise she-bee who had done so well in training and nurturing her. She knew this might be goodbye, so she kissed the small bee's forehead tenderly before tearing her gaze away. With sorrow, she coursed on to the throne room. She needed to tell Amber what she was feeling right away.

Royal was also in decline, which was of course expected with her age. But it didn't make a moment like this any less scary. With new and inexperienced leadership, Sugar only hoped they could face whatever lay before them. Royal and others had worked so hard to bring this hive from its torment into its freedom. They couldn't let that all go. It had to amount to something, to a peace that could last.

But not yet.

She entered the throne room with fervor. "Queen Amber, we need to talk!"

The young Queen jumped in surprise. "Sugar! You never cease to… give me a thrill!" She smiled faintly. The two had only been working together for a few weeks and their dynamic was still developing. Overall, they functioned fine together and were doing a good job with the day-to-day functions of the hive, but sometimes Sugar was so straightforward that it startled Amber.

The doors closed behind her, and Sugar spoke with urgency. "Something is coming today. Something dark and powerful. We must prepare immediately."

Amber looked stunned. "Wait… I have so many questions. What do you mean something dark and powerful? How are we to respond?"

Sugar buzzed, "Troops. We need to get ready for the fight of our lives."

The young Queen's eyes darted around in sheer panic. Taking a slow breath, Sugar reflected on how well Nectar worked with Royal. The nurse bee had always been able to share her inclinations while simultaneously putting her queen's heart at ease. Sugar had often marveled at her grace in such things. She knew she needed to try her best to do the same in this moment. "I have mentioned before that we suspected a threat building, and in response we had prepared for such a day to come. Let's put that in motion now. With the Light on our side, I know we can protect you and our home. I have a feeling that once this threat is eliminated, that peace we've been glimpsing will be a lasting reward."

The Queen grew visibly calmer. She took a breath to collect herself and her thoughts before starting to deliver orders to nearby servants. Within moments, the word was being spread to all. Amber looked at Sugar curiously.

"How do you know these things with such certainty?"

Sugar smiled briefly. "The Light guides me, Your Majesty. Now, stay safe at the back of the hive with protection. You are key to our survival. I will also join you after delivering the news to a few other leaders."

With an approving nod, Amber dismissed Sugar to her tasks. The young nurse bee charged through the hive with hardly disguised urgency, making her way to the landing grounds and entrance. She peered out, prudently searching for anything unusual. So far, there was nothing of concern to be seen. A few bees nearby watched her with piqued interest.

"What's the matter Sugar?" One worker called.

Sugar turned to them. "Spread the message. We expect a threat at some point today. Stop all pollinating and focus on hive defense."

The worker stared in shock, and Sugar dismissed herself quickly. She hurried her way to Courage's mentorship cell at the edge of the grounds and knocked. He opened the door.

"Oh hi, Sugar! I'm in session... is something wrong?" Courage tilted his head as he tried to read the nurse bee's expression. He grew concerned. "It's time?"

"I believe so. Today, we will be attacked. Stop all usual daily tasks and be prepared for hive defense." Sugar looked at Courage meaningfully. "I think it's Buzzz."

The drone's face hardened with resolve. In the room with him, Theo had been in session with Courage. His faced reflected sheer terror and he started to panic.

"No! I'll be the first one he kills!"

Courage turned to help calm Theo down, nodding respectfully at Sugar to let her go. The nurse bee was off, and even in the short time she spoke with Courage, it was clear that the hive was more aware. Bees sprinted in every direction. Some were panicked while others were dutifully attending to whatever task they had to perform. Some adventurer and fighter bees had gathered near the entrance to start patrols. Doctor and caregiver bees gathered supplies and cleared space to treat potentially wounded hivemates. Others were stretching their wings and limbs in preparation for a battle, or grabbing a snack before what lay ahead.

Sugar felt a tiny daunting feeling inside. *What if I'm wrong?* She looked around, suddenly self-conscious. Her role in this hive was young and untested. *No... I know what I'm feeling.* She clenched her jaw with determination and started her way back to Queen Amber. *I have to protect her. I have to be right by her side.*

Chapter 12: Preparations

The sky was a bit gloomy today and the wind had a chill to it. Joy shuddered as a gust hit her in flight. She had taken it upon herself to join a hive patrol as soon as she heard the news, and other enemy researchers had encouraged her to partake. By now, Joy was one of the most knowledgeable of the group; her passion had fueled her to learn extremely fast and well. On top of that, she'd had some fighting instruction in her free time recently, so she figured she'd be able to hold her own.

The patrols were meant to be small, fast, and undetected. The eight bees signaled quietly amongst one another to proceed from tree trunk to tree trunk. So far, they didn't see anything unusual or alarming, and they had quickly reached the northwestern edge of Shadow Forest. Joy peered into Alfalfa Field with great effort, trying to make something out of the vast, bleary openness. Nothing. But still, she was on edge. *Something is wrong here.* The patrol ended up looping back to return to the hive, where a whole schedule of patrols were ready to trade off in different locations.

As they snuck through the forest, it wasn't too long before the hive came into sight. The eight bees relaxed at the sight of their home and became careless. Joy suddenly noticed movement in the corner of her eye, and a moment later, one of her hivemates was gone. Then another. She looked around in shock, and it seemed like some of the patrol hadn't even noticed. Another was taken. Now only 5 remained.

Joy quickly changed direction in midair, as did the other four who had now noticed the disturbance. Unfortunately, one of them was too late, and was swept away. But this time, Joy witnessed the attacker. She made a great effort to keep her eyes on that blur until it disappeared behind a tree branch. Whatever the creature was, it was smart, and it didn't seem to look like a honey bee.

Joy locked right into action. She made her way carefully and discreetly to a place where she might observe the creature at rest. She crawled quietly up a tree trunk rather than flying, and once safely crouched above the particular branch, looked down. The sight was rather appalling.

A ghastly observation it certainly was to see one's comrade torn to bits. Trying to focus on the creature rather than the horrible sight, Joy's eyes sparked with recognition. There crouched a long and lean abdomen, hairless and sleek. It had several narrow yellow and black stripes on its back, and two long athletic wings that shimmered. She moved her gaze reluctantly to the front of the creature. Bold yellow markings shone around its chiseled cheek, and long black antennae waved around with glee. The creature's tapered jaw led to intimidating hooked mandibles, of which tore easily through its prey. Joy shuddered. *Yellowjackets.*

She immediately knew she needed to warn the hive, so she started a stealthy and unusual path back to the hive entrance. *It's likely she isn't the only one.* She reflected on her knowledge of yellowjackets. While they weren't usually a giant threat to honey bees, they certainly could be if the hive were weak or surprised. Most of the time, yellowjackets might hover near a hive to catch a few bees for lunch. But in worse cases, they could invade a hive and pillage its contents. They could even destroy a hive in the worst case scenario.

Her eyes darted around, watching closely for any movements in her peripheral vision. Her journey felt long and precarious. It was about ten minutes before she was at the foot of the hive on the forest floor, and she began climbing up toward the hive entrance. At this point, the yellowjackets were still undetected by the hive, and a new patrol was just about to leave.

"Wait!" Joy gasped as she passed through the entrance. A few groups of bees near the doors turned to her, curious. She took a huge sigh as her body relaxed in the safety of the hive. "Listen, I'm an Enemy Researcher. I went on a patrol to the forest edge and on our way back, several of my party were picked off by... yellowjackets."

The listeners gasped.

"We really need to be careful! Yellowjackets are stealthy. They will continue to pick us off if we aren't attentive. I saw one for myself. But where there's one, there are likely to be others. We need to stand guard and prepare ourselves in case there's a bigger swarm."

King Sting parted through the crowd to where Joy stood. His face looked weary and sad, but he held himself strong nonetheless, ready to lead his hive. "What is your name, worker?"

"Joy. I'm an Enemy Researcher." She straightened a bit shyly.

"Yellowjackets you say? We need to know more. What kind of threat are we dealing with?"

Joy paused. "Often, yellowjackets will hang out around beehives in small numbers to pick off a bee here or there. Normally they won't dare to try and enter. But pairing this with our nurse bee's warnings, we should be prepared for the possibility of a greater danger. At their worst, large groups of yellowjackets have attempted to infiltrate hives. Usually they only pick on weaker ones. They can pillage our food stores, destroy our nurseries, and kill bees. If we aren't prepared, it can be devastating. They have been known to even kill Queens, wipe out entire hives, and keep honey stores to themselves." She let out a nervous breath.

Sting stared at her with resolve. "Thank you for this information. We will need your expertise as we handle this." The King turned to shout orders to various groups and leaders before turning back to Joy. "Stay with leadership when you can; we'll benefit from your advice."

Joy had many emotions. For one, the hive was facing danger today, and she had seen hivemates being stolen by these creatures. But now, she was able to use the knowledge in her head to help the hive, and that was admittedly exhilarating. *I will do whatever I can to equip us for the dangers ahead!*

QUEEN AMBER WAS OVERWHELMED. In all the newness of being a Queen, she felt helpless to handle the situation at hand. But during the day, she had spent most of her time seeking counsel from Queen Royal as she lay in bed. The poor old Queen was declining rapidly. The last talk they had, Royal had urged her to assign leaders and plans for communication. This way, she wouldn't be managing the possible battle alone. After sharing this, the old Queen had turned over and fallen into an uneasy sleep.

Amber had thought about this long and hard, consulting with Sugar and Sting when possible. After some time, she decided what roles needed to be filled and by whom. She recently sent her attendants to fetch Sting and a few others, and after a while they were knocking on her door.

"Come in." Before her stood Sting, Sugar, Courage, and several workers from specific professions in the hive. Amber's King, Justice, was at her side as well and eager to help facilitate things. *He is a confident and eager drone, but maybe a bit quick to take risks.* Taking a breath, she began to speak. "Hive Honey Quest needs organization at a time such as this. Sting, Royal, and Justice have given me a lot of good counsel, and I have made my decisions."

The noble bees before her dipped their heads and listened respectfully as she continued. "Sting, you will be our highest general on the battlefield. Your experience, training, and level-headed approach is unmatched. I have also decided to instate Courage as a high general, just beneath you. He can help advise you and lead other groups of bees. Both of you will report to me and King Justice through messengers. We trust your decision making skills, but try to communicate everything you can." Courage appeared surprised and honored to bear such a position, and the two drones nodded toward each other.

Amber looked at the workers she'd summoned. There was a lead doctor bee, a couple of lead nurse bees, an experienced adventurer, two highly-ranked fighters, an old guard drone, and two caretakers. "You all will hold positions of management in your departments. Doctor bees will stay at our home base to care for the wounded. We need to set up and designate an area of the hive specifically for this. Some nurses will stay here as well, while others will need to go as scouts on the battlefield. Their job will be to bring our wounded home for care, or do emergency medicine immediately as needed. You three can be dismissed to begin these preparations and organize a working system among your specialties."

The doctor and nurse bees dipped their heads with serious expressions and took off at her command. Amber continued. "Adventurers are my chosen specialty to handle communications. You may have the help of explorers as well, if this battle leaves our home base. You will supervise and manage your specialty, choosing who to appoint and where to send them. Send bees who can take unusual but efficient paths so as to avoid a clash with the enemy. These bees will need to patrol between generals and captains from start to finish, and we don't want any fatalities."

The head Adventurer bowed before the Queen dismissed her. "Next, the guard. Sir, you are the overseer of protection at our hive's entrance. There will be many guards and fighters under your command. You need to do everything you can to protect our home base from invasion. As for fighters, you two will help manage subgroups in battle. Train bees whenever the pace slows down, and be sure to keep our entrance heavily guarded. You will answer to the lead guard, and he will answer to our generals."

The guard acknowledged the Queen's words with a fierce grunt, and the three departed. The last group to remain were the two caretaker she-bees. They looked at their Queen expectantly. "Caretakers will be the head of supplies. Your jobs will include overseeing the delivery of various needs to both the wounded and the army. At first, you'll need to focus around equipment and herbs. But if this battle goes on for a while, you'll need to help support our army's stomachs. Honey deliveries may become necessary, for both drones who can't pollinate, and for any groups who are in more desolate or hidden areas. We must stay fed and strong. You may find yourselves collaborating with messengers often, which will help keep you and the supplies safe. Make sure there are also fighters attending you."

With that, the Queen dismissed the workers, and the only bees remaining were Sting, Courage, Sugar, herself, and King Justice. Amber took a long breath after so much delegating, and rested into her chair.

Justice was eager to talk with the drones. "Men, have there been any developments on the yellowjacket situation since you last reported?"

Sting stood tall. "Yes, which reminds me of someone else we'll need to appoint. I was speaking with the young bee Joy, and she has quickly become the most knowledgeable enemy researcher in the hive. I wish to appoint her to lead in interspecies situations. She was able to clue me in on yellowjacket behavior. If we can understand our interspecies enemies better, we will be much better off. I want her to advise Courage and I as we lead."

King Justice agreed. "You're right, Sting. Understanding our enemies will be extremely important, especially since this is one of very few instances we've dealt with other species."

Courage looked pleased to hear about his sister's appointment, and Sting continued. "Yellowjacket behavior hasn't changed since it started, but we are on the lookout constantly to watch for a shift. We've notified all patrols to work differently and be especially watchful. We've been unable to observe the yellowjackets' reaction to this, because they are staying hidden."

King Justice looked satisfied. Eyeing Courage, he asked, "Young drone, are you equipped and prepared to handle this degree of leadership?"

"I am." Courage answered quickly, with an air of true confidence and a stable mind. "I will not let you down."

Sting smiled. "Courage is ready. He's had great responsibility from his early days, and his mind is a steel trap. I have full confidence entrusting bees under his guidance." Turning to the young drone, he continued. "You will lead many fighters on the front lines. I will stay closer to home to make sure things are running as they should at the hive and entrance."

King Justice spoke again. "I want you generals to utilize the chute. For as long as it isn't discovered by our enemies, it will be a discreet way for one or two bees at a time to slip away to their tasks. Don't draw attention to it, but it will also be guarded." He paused. "Send messengers to report on any further developments, and stay on the field. The Queen and I will stay here in safety, protected by Sugar and a good sized group of fierce defenders."

The nurse bee, having stayed quiet for some time to absorb everything, perked up at the mention of her name. "Yes. I need to stay with the lifeblood of our hive. I won't be in and out much. I've arranged for Nectar to be transported to Royal's quarters next to us as well, and she should be arriving shortly. Both she-bees are failing quickly and must be protected beside our Queen."

Everyone nodded in agreement. Then, Sugar spoke again. "If we are done here, I'm feeling a strong sense that a change is occurring. We need to settle into our roles with haste."

"So no false alarm?" Queen Amber offered with bitter humor.

"No. No false alarm."

Chapter 13: Strategy

"**A**re we just gonna sit and wait while they pick us off? Or are we gonna do something?"

"We should wait. We have no idea how many there are or where they're hiding."

The panic and stress at the hive entrance was building while Sting was away speaking to Queen Amber. Now, the two generals were returning to sort things out and prepare for battle. Courage was surprised by how natural he felt in this new position. His mind was already working on how to approach things strategically, and he was filled with resolve.

"We'll have the advantage of equilibrium and organization now." Courage offered to Sting. "How do you want to act?"

"We need to see first if anything has changed like Sugar announced. Then, we'll weigh our options before we act." The gathering settled as the old retired king entered the landing grounds, and they looked to him with expectation and hope. Sting acknowledged them, but didn't say a word before speaking with the hive guard in command. Courage came with.

"Any changes?" Sting asked.

The old drone stood firmly. "Yes. We are seeing them now. The yellowjackets have increased significantly in number and are purposely exposing themselves to us now and then. It appears that they are trying to draw us outside."

Sting nodded quickly. "Thank you." Turning to Courage, he thought out loud. "Based on Joy's description of yellowjacket behavior patterns, this is unusual for them. Still, I feel confident in saying their goal is to infiltrate our hive. This theory is strengthened by the fact that their numbers are growing as we speak. They seem to want to weaken and separate us. But at the same time, they may continue to grow in numbers until they take the hive by force if we don't act in some way."

Courage nodded thoughtfully. "Possible responses seem to be: hunker down and stay unified until we understand their ranks better, or send out a small but mighty and stealthy crew to gather information more quickly. A crew that can possibly go unnoticed. Other than that, what are our options?"

Sting contemplated. "We should use their hesitation to our advantage. We need to send a discreet messenger out through the chute to notify our allies, the wild hive. This messenger should know our early plans and convey them upon arrival. Secondly, we are still finding our footing in the organization department. I want to wait just a little longer before we make a move on the offense. I also want two small groups composed of both adventurers and explorers to search for any other enemies beyond the wood. They'll also use the chute to depart discreetly. After sending off those missions, we should avoid using the chute for a while, and beef up its defenses."

Courage nodded. "I think you are right to air on the side of patience right now while we find a sturdy footing. But how long will we wait?"

"Until something changes, I think it would be foolish to throw ourselves at a dormant hovering enemy. That might be giving them exactly what they want, and could weaken our troops. So far, they've been trying to thin us out one by one. They probably expect to continue doing so as a way to weaken us before the war even escalates. I will have us remain strong and unified until we are provoked into action."

"At least we know this isn't just another mild predator threat. Sugar's insight tells us that this is part of something bigger. The yellowjackets probably want us to believe that they are a small and singular threat."

"Yes," Sting responded, "they should have no idea that we see past them now. Good observation, rookie." The retired king shouldered

Courage with a decisive glimmer in his eye. "Let's go set some things in motion and communicate to the troops."

As the drones approached the crowd, Joy broke through. "Sting! Oh, Courage, hi!" The bright young worker was determined and sharp in her expression.

"Joy. Hive leadership have agreed to appoint you as head of your specialty and an advisor to myself and General Courage." Sting buzzed.

Joy looked at Courage, appearing shocked and pleased. "Wow, brother! Look at us!" She smiled, before becoming serious. "I'm certain you know this, but female yellowjackets can sting. And they aren't limited. They can sting and sting again just like a Queen bee." Her face darkened. "While their jaws are scary enough, all of our troops need to keep this in mind to protect themselves. I'm afraid that without any kind of weapon, we'll be powerless to defend against a swarm of them."

Sting considered this. "Yes, thank you Joy. Weapons... we should ask the wild hive to bring their stinger covers for workers to use. As for us drones, we should use weapons as well. Rose thorns and sharp twigs could be helpful. Although we don't have many in storage, I'll send someone to distribute whatever we have right away."

Courage perked up. "Hey, New Beginning had a stash of those in their corner of the hive. I think we left them there. We should utilize those as well."

"Very good!"

The three bees began to put their thoughts into action. Hive Honey Quest was more prepared than could be expected in such a scenario, and though their King and Queen were young, their armies were in position to be a formidable opponent.

As the hive was quietly preparing, small ranks of yellowjackets huffed in frustration outside.

"Ughhhhhzz!" A brilliantly striped female hissed behind a tree trunk. "Where are zzheeyyy?"

"Hush!" The large drone who led the yellowjackets, Hissgaar, was nearby as well. "Zheyy will not be zzzimple opponentzzz. Zzzhey are of Buzzz's line. Paitenczzzeee."

The worker scoffed with scorn. "When doezzzz Buzzz move in?"

"Szzzooon, worker. Be zzzstill."

BUZZZ TOOK A STEADY and determined breath. He looked proudly over the ranks of honey bees before him who were ready to depart. In a short time, their numbers had grown significantly enough to be a real threat. He paced back and forth, sizing up a new worker or drone with each pass. *They need to know who they answer to.* Buzzz had supervised the preparation and gathering of his ranks while Hissgaar paved his path with some of the yellowjackets. Now, he was simply awaiting the cue to depart and close in on Hive Honey Quest.

Deep in thought, he almost hadn't noticed the queen bee Amethyst creeping out of her cell. She stared almost woefully at her brood, trepidation in her eyes. Crawling to Buzzz's feet, she spoke with a serious tone. "Dear, are you certain that this is the only way to build our future? I fear many of our offspring will be lost."

Buzzz turned his face toward her with a cold expression. "We will make more." He didn't have the brainpower to care right now. He was busy strategizing and eagerly awaiting his signal.

"Oh! How can you say that with such little care?" The queen groveled pathetically, starting to cry. "Each bee is special."

Buzzz scoffed, impatient. He took a breath to stabilize himself. *I can't lose her right now.* He turned toward her, allowing his eyes to soften. "Sometimes doing the right thing costs us greatly. I'm ready to do that in order to secure our future, no matter how grave the losses may be." He paused, his expression changing to become more critical. "Do you think I'm unfit to make the right decision for our troops? Do you have that little faith in me?"

Amethyst looked up at him, her eyes wide. "No, no my King! I'm so sorry, I never meant to question you..."

"Good, then let me do my job. I can assure you that our offspring are in good hands." He gently brushed her away from his side, allowing her to revel in her regret for questioning him. How Buzzz interacted with Amethyst was all extremely strategic, just like his next moves would be. The drone was quite good at strategizing across the board. He took a sigh, content with his management, when suddenly a yellowjacket burst into his hollow.

"Buzzz, it izzzz time." The messenger gave Buzzz some updates on how things had progressed thus far, which wasn't necessarily as they had hoped and planned for.

A fire lit in his eyes and his belly. Buzzz's thirst for revenge and atonement was stronger than ever, and it *would* finally have its way no matter what setbacks they may have. "Drones and workers, rise! We are off to take back what is rightfully ours!" With that, they began to swarm.

Chapter 14: Infiltration

Courage paced the landing grounds with anticipation. *This is it, I can feel it. This is the final reason I am here again with Hive Honey Quest.* The drone, though young in months, exuded an air of one much older and wiser. He watched as troops of bees found their bearings in the clearing and instructions were being communicated clearly to all. *I will help lead us out of this into true victory. Then, there will be a great stretch of rest and joy to follow. At last, the hive will be free of turmoil. Their souls will be at peace, and stronger than ever.*

Just then, Courage felt a great weight of urgency and warning upon his spirit. "Sting!" Courage called to the hive's old king across the grounds, and he turned toward Courage. In a moment, his face changed. Before anybee could even respond, they found themselves being heavily attacked.

In through the guarded entrance of the hive streamed more yellowjackets than they could count. The powerful winged creatures plowed through the main gate like a dark plague. Without hesitation, Sting gestured his commands. Several large troops of bees attempted to isolate the large creatures and eliminate them, but as they poured in, their numbers had grown to a dangerous level quickly.

Courage hurried to Sting's side through the chaos. The old drone spoke quickly and clearly. "Take half of our troops and go immediately through the reduced edge of the entrance. Stop the flow of yellowjackets coming in so that I can have the rest of the hive entrance reduced and sealed immediately."

"Sealed?" Worry rose up in Courage's chest, but there was no time to question Sting's command. Courage flung himself into a mass of Hive Honey Quest's soldiers that waited for directions. He spread the message quickly and before long, about half of the hive's troops were filing out of the narrow edge of the entrance not suitable for yellowjackets. Glancing back, he locked eyes with Sting, who nodded quickly in acknowledgment. Courage didn't have time to hesitate. He left the hive and with a piercing battle cry to disrupt the stream of yellowjackets. To his horror, there was a massive swarm still hovering to enter the hive. Many of the entrance guard bees had already been trampled and thrown to the side without much effort.

Courage signaled to his army and soon, they were forming a powerful, tight-knit swarm at the hive entrance. Temporarily, the flow of yellowjackets into the hive was forced to cease. Immediately after stopping the flow, he heard the sound of hundreds of honey bees sealing off the hive behind him. Courage shrieked and fiercely battered the giant creatures before him with an almost supernatural vigor. His mind entered a place of ultimate focus and strength. It was almost as if he was no longer functioning from his own body and energy. Instead, an unshakable power poured through him, and he was a fierce opponent.

Yellowjackets were nasty enemies. Around him, many bees were stung or dismembered by powerful jaws. Still, he charged on with the strength of multiple bees. He held his ground, constantly aware of the sound of work happening at the hive entrance. Time was an odd thing when in combat. It could have been a minute or it could have been forever, but soon Courage heard a few dull thuds. *The hive is sealed. Now we must break away and regroup.*

Signaling to his troops, they suddenly and quickly dispersed, much to the yellowjackets' confusion. The enemies hesitated, blinking in awe at the sealed entrance. Courage took advantage of their hesitation and much of his army was able to melt away without a challenge. Courage stealthily made his way to the location he had signaled to his troops - a well-hidden, hollowed old trunk just far enough away to safely regroup. *I hope I will have an army.* Courage couldn't be sure just how many bees would make it to safety after their brazen defense.

He took a moment to process what had just happened.

A war had officially begun, and at this moment, the hive's entire livelihood was at stake. Their home was infiltrated with several dangerous predators. Sting had ordered the sealing of the hive as a way to protect them from further danger, and this did make sense. Still, it was terrifying to imagine being trapped in a vulnerable place with countless powerful enemies and no escape. And now, Courage was the only leader outside. He would be responsible for stewarding the troops alone, and for guiding the wild hive when they'd arrive soon. It was all on him.

Courage made it to the hollowed trunk. Looking around, he saw a decent number of stragglers already there. More joined them as he watched. *Not many yet. We'll soon see where we stand.* Workers and drones around him turned their attention to their leader as they waited to regroup. Courage sat silently for about ten minutes, after gesturing for the army to be at ease. To his relief, many more bees found their way to the hidden location and a sizable crowd was forming. As some of what appeared to be the last stragglers trickled in, an old drone buzzed loudly.

"Buzzz has been sighted!" He gasped for breath. "He is here. Sugar was right. Buzzz has returned!"

Courage quietly made his way toward the drone. "When was he seen?"

"I saw him and a small swarm of honey bees approaching the edge of the forest just as I slipped away from the hive entrance. I was one of the last to get away. I made sure he didn't see me while I investigated and then fled."

"And you are sure it was him?"

"Yes." The old drone's expression was sobering. "I will never forget how Buzzz flies."

Courage nodded in gratitude. "Thank you." The young general parted his way through the crowd toward the front, his hive-mates looking on expectantly. He was their leader, after all. It seemed that most had been able to gather their wits. Thanks to Sugar's heads up, the whole hive had been able to mentally prepare for something like this to happen. At the front of the space, Courage gathered himself. He signaled for everybee's attention.

"Hive Honey Quest! The foretold battle has arrived. Don't fear. Sting and others have had time to arrange for a working system when it comes to communication, supplies, and a starting point. I will stand proudly by you all, as we valiantly fight to protect our hive from harm. Winning this war will mean that we can finally be free from torment. Physical and spiritual peace will resound for generations." The crowd buzzed in wonder. "But, we have to fight, and win. You must stand strong to defend our home and the things you love. You and I are outside of the hive. We might run into Buzzz or other leaders. We don't know how many wait to kill us out here. But we will also have the wild hive's help. Take heart, and be attentive to my lead. I believe that Lighthive will give us victory!"

The crowd cheered. Parting her way toward Courage, a worker cried out. "Brother!" It was Joy. Courage gasped in delight and gave her a hug.

"You're okay!" He smiled.

"I am!" Joy stayed silent then, respecting her brother's leadership as the crowd quieted.

"We need to make camp. I'll be sending out some groups to scout for Buzzz, gather information, and keep watch for the wild hive. But for now, be at rest and gather your strength. This has all just begun." The sun was getting low in the sky and night was approaching. Courage shuddered at the thought of what might be happening inside the hive. *Lighthive, be with Sting and my hivemates. Give them strength. Be with our new Queen, and protect her.* As his troops began making preparations to get some rest, Courage turned toward his sister.

"You were born to lead, Courage." She smiled sadly at him. "But, I'm scared. Yellowjackets are no small threat, especially the number we observed at the hive. By nature's law, we should all be dead already, and the chances for our queen are very slim."

Courage looked at her, his eyes glittering with mist. "Trust in the Light, sister. Hold fast. We are Hive Honey Quest. We won't be going down without the fight of our lives."

Joy took a breath of resolve. "How can I help?"

"I would like for you to help me arrange the groups for patrols and night watches. Also, we need to have a plan for sustenance. I believe many of the bees who were assigned the responsibility of keeping us fed are currently confined to the hive. We don't know how long the hive will be sealed. So we need to decide where and when our bees can feed."

Joy nodded quickly. "Let's start."

INSIDE HIVE HONEY QUEST, there was no rest for the weary. It was like something out of a nightmare. Many yellowjackets had made it inside before the hive was sealed, and countless bees had already fallen victim to the formidable creatures. Sting's body ached as the endless battle continued. His only hope at the moment was getting to the stash of weapons within the hive. Unfortunately, most of the hive's weapons hadn't been obtained or distributed just yet.

He had been inching his way toward the old meeting place for New Beginning, in which he knew some of the weapons were stored. *The survival of the hive depends on this.* He told himself the same thing over and over, determined to stay alive and not give up. His old joints were screaming and threatening to collapse, but he pressed on. Suddenly, he saw his opportunity to slip away unnoticed by his enemies. He was finally able to sneak off and strengthen his army.

Quietly and stealthily, he flew through the halls that the yellowjackets had not yet taken to find the weapons. He made it there without being detected. Having no idea what weapons would be there or how many, he held his breath as he opened the storage room door. Before him hung a good number of twig spears and rose thorns. *Good! This will help!* He took as many as he could carry and made his way back to the edge of his forces for them to be distributed. A few others came with him for a second trip, and before long, they cleaned out the room.

"Make sure to use the thorns by hand rather than throwing. We must not risk the enemies getting their hands on these. They already have more powerful biological weapons. Carry the thorns concealed in the battlefield, using them discreetly when necessary. Distribute the spears to the edges where protection is most important. Bring some to the guards at the chute and the throne room at the back of the hive." His attendants nodded, grateful for their leader's straightforward commands.

It was when the weapons were distributed that the battle started to change. The yellowjackets were fierce and aggressive, and the concealed thorns served well against such brazen strategies. The large creatures yowled in frustration, unable to see or understand why they were losing the upper hand. For maybe an hour, the battle continued in this way. Slowly, the number of yellowjackets was diminishing.

Sting knew the troops needed rest. He arranged for guards and outer ring soldiers to rotate with the front lines. Honey bees were quite good at nonverbal communication, and they operated as a well-oiled machine. Sting stayed out of the front lines at this point, making sure that operations were going on as desired. He knew they needed to keep at it if they wanted to survive.

The sun was setting and the hive grew quite dark. The yellowjackets began to catch on to the use of weapons and started to fight with more caution. A large group of them even pulled back to regroup in the landing grounds, giving a pause for the troops to breathe. It was an eerie and unsafe feeling to crouch in waiting. This was the bees' home, and it was where they were usually the most safe. Now, they were at their most vulnerable. The yellowjackets were likely to change their strategy, and Sting knew he had to keep a close eye out for them.

In a moment of silence and darkness, he began to hear sounds near the outer comb. Sting immediately knew what to be concerned about based on Joy's prior guidance. *"Usually if yellowjackets are able to enter a hive, they will try to desecrate our brood and steal our food."* Sting thought of the nursery comb. *We need to protect our young if we can.* Sting set off right away to assign a small part of his army to the task.

Chapter 15: To Lie In Wait

Buzzz yowled in frustration. *They sealed the hive?!* He had to admit, it was a wise strategy. Hive Honey Quest had put a halt to the strength of Buzzz's infiltration plans. Now, he found himself and his army hovering outside the hive, hesitant.

One of his daughters nearby asked sheepishly, "What should we do?"

"Some of you, go now and listen at the sealed entrance. Tell me if it is guarded or unguarded." The she-bee and others took off right away, and Buzzz waited. *I expect it's guarded. But if there is even one small unprotected section, we can quietly eat our way in through small holes and strengthen the numbers within.*

The worker shook her head after they listened. Flying back to Buzzz, she reported. "There is plenty of bustle right by the entrance at every section."

"Let us check the chute." Buzzz led his army toward the side of the hive without hesitation. While the yellowjackets and other natural predators may not know about the chute, Buzzz did. He knew about every nook and cranny of the hive, and any possible entrance or hidden room. As he approached the chute, he was horrified to see it stuffed full with the bodies of yellowjackets. *They must be fighting stronger than expected.* He took a moment to think.

"We will establish a headquarters and regroup. If anyone from Hive Honey Quest is outside, we will destroy them." Wordlessly, he turned toward the woods. His troops followed him as he made his way to a familiar rosebush. He furrowed his brow as the flashbacks came. Hope had almost killed him that day during the War of the Ghost. He had gotten a nasty scar to show for it. *She had better be dead, or she'll regret that she's still living.*

Within a few minutes of sprinting, they made it to the bush. Buzzz signaled for all to conceal themselves within the thorny branches immediately, and they listened. He took a moment to pace and brood. *I've always known the hive has wits. But it seems like nothing is going quite right.* Buzzz could only hope that the yellowjackets were succeeding within the hive walls. After a few minutes, he gave orders to his troops.

"Send out patrols. We need to see if anybee lingers outside the hive. Whoever we find will be our focus for now. Meanwhile, I want some of you waiting outside the hive entrance constantly listening for a breach. If you notice a lull, one of you must report to this bush immediately while the others begin to destroy the seal."

After his orders began to unfold, Buzzz took a long frustrated sigh and settled on a branch. As a leader in battle, he wouldn't put himself on the front lines where he actually preferred to be. He would be settled at the headquarters managing his troops. Just as he was getting antsy, he heard the strange chortle of Hissgaar's frustrated buzzing.

He turned to see the giant yellowjacket drone standing nearby. Hissgaar spoke. "My troopzzzz are zzplit up. Half made it inzzzzide and half are withzz me."

Buzzz nodded slowly.

The tall insect hissed, suddenly enraged, and smashed a fist onto the branch Buzzz was sitting on. "I szzzwear, if my entire crew izzzz destroyed, you szzzhould be ready to compenszzate!"

"Are you threatening me, Hissgaar?" Buzz stood, boldly staring down his ally. "Because I distinctly remember that the terms of this arrangement have already been agreed upon AND satisfied."

The yellowjacket didn't shrink away. "You zzzeem to think zhat yellowjacketzzzzz alwayzzz play fair."

Buzzz glared intently as Hissgaar. "Believe me. If you were to break our agreement, I myself wouldn't hold back. You have no idea what you'd be facing." A sick fire burned in Buzzz's eyes, and it caused Hissgaar to flinch for just a moment.

Buzzz had established good rapport with dark forces, and fully believed they would enable him to do anything. They would make sure he won this war and that he'd maintain superiority. This intense certainty gave him an edge in all dealings with others, as his eyes burned with the strength of darkness. His mind was sharp with the wit of its deception, manipulation, and persuasion.

After an uneasy moment, the yellowjacket relaxed his stature a bit and dipped his head respectfully at Buzzz. "Tzzzell me your planzzz."

THE NIGHT OUTSIDE WAS long and suspenseful, but no battles occurred before the sun began making its appearance again. Courage managed to get some sleep, while light and troubled it was. It must have been dawn when he stirred. A worker from the early morning watch had gently woken him up. He jumped, on edge, but relaxed when he saw her. "What is it?"

"Good news. I believe our allies have arrived."

Courage perked up. "Oh good! Show me to them!" They quietly wove between camps of sleeping bees to the edge of their quarters. There, Courage saw a Soldier. He appeared to be of high status - possibly a leader of their group. The rest of the allies were nowhere to be seen.

Courage dipped his head, an expression of gratitude on his face. "Thank you for coming. Sir..."

"I am Sir Keen. I am the leading general overseeing this mission." The soldier must have noticed Courage looking around, searching for the troops. "Ah, my hivemates are present as well. We brought good numbers. They are perched in the shadows on the trunk. Is there room for us to join your ranks?"

Courage nodded. "Yes, of course. It's time for my army to wake, so don't worry about any commotion." He gestured to welcome Sir Keen and his crew into their base, and he blinked in surprise as bees filed in. They marched in organized lines, and those rows just kept on coming. Almost immediately, the camp was stirring. Exclamations of new hope and confidence broke out here and there as everybee realized what was going on.

After a while, all of Courage's and Sir Keen's troops were packed together. They made up a sizable crowd. The last several soldiers to file in carried sacks of stinger covers with them, and those were quickly distributed to eligible fighters.

Around then, a patrol reached the base, and a worker reported to Courage. "We believe we know where Buzzz's swarm has settled. There is also new activity at the hive entrance. Foreign honey bees hover there. So far, they've only been lurking. Nothing else."

"Thank you!" Courage paused, contemplative. "Where has Buzzz settled?"

"He is in a large rosebush to the west, we think. We also saw a few yellowjackets around the area. I don't believe we were detected."

"Excellent work!" Courage dismissed the worker with a smile. *That rosebush sounds familiar.* Courage had been trained on the War of the Ghost, and Thistle and Iris had shown him most of the notable landmarks. *Chances are, it's the same location.* He then thought about the bees at the hive. Dread filled his belly, having no updates on the status inside. Either way, he figured he should respond to the activity there. Maybe he would be able to get some new information on Sting, the hive, and the Queen's safety.

Courage went ahead and arranged various small missions for certain patrols, including scouting the hive entrance and the rosebush headquarters. Beyond that, he felt a bit uneasy having such a large group of bees crouching in one small space, so he sent some bees to seek out nearby places for some of the army to remain more hidden while they awaited their own directions. *That way, if our base is discovered and ambushed, we will have the advantage to protect ourselves.*

After a very busy dawn, Courage took a moment for himself to sit and breathe. Leading others was a great responsibility. While he felt capable of the role, he felt the great pressure of it. He knew that his word could send bees to their deaths. His success could bring victory, and his failure could bring destruction. He bore a heavy weight on his shoulders. *Lighthive, take control. May I be your vessel.* He took some deep breaths as he centered himself, and before long the pressure on his shoulders began to lift. He clicked into a mode of sorts, where every action he made would flow from a strength within. He wasn't alone in this. With renewed determination, he stood tall. His expression was confident and capable, but not lacking warmth. He was full of wisdom and humility. Anybee who saw him was blown away by the perfection of his countenance - a way of functioning that could only flow directly from the Light.

It was through times like this that Courage felt most aligned with the truth. He could step into the embrace of Lighthive despite the uncertainty of circumstances. No matter what happened to his physical body in battle, he could charge on in total trust of the truth. He was ready to sacrifice everything for this cause he was called to, and he was even more ready to help pick up the pieces if they (Lighthive willing) could pull through and achieve victory. He had a deep and unwavering knowing that no matter what, all would be well and Lighthive would continue to reign supreme.

Chapter 16: Regicide and Extrication

After a great lull full of suspense, the storm of battle was about to build simultaneously. It was late morning when within Hive Honey Quest, the noise at the entrance was settling. Buzzz's scouts took advantage of this and immediately began tearing into the entrance. Reinforcements from Buzzz's troops arrived with great haste. Sting and his ranks had been battered in nearly constant battle, with very little energy left. Many had been wounded or lost, but many yellowjackets had also been killed. Outside, yellowjacket buzzing became the dominant sound as they made their numbers known throughout the forest. It was clear that they did not feel threatened, and their sheer numbers were staggering. Several groups of Soldiers and Hive Honey Quest bees lay in hiding, waiting for the time they would be needed. Many of Courage's troops were positioned to attack the rosebush after having gathered enough information, and others were positioned to help at the hive.

All at once, the true war commenced. With a startling crack, the last of the hive entrance blockage was forced away and Buzzz's troops began pushing through the gap single-file. At the same time, many of Sting's troops began filing out of the recently cleared chute. They took refuge in the grass, their bodies aching with tiredness. It was only moments before Courage was able to respond, thanks to his watchful patrols. He himself came to join the exhausted bees.

Sting was with them. At the sight of Courage, he perked up. "Thank goodness, you're okay!"

"I should say the same about you!" Courage buzzed. Sting's expression grew dark.

"Many of us are no more."

"The queen?" Courage asked, his eyes showing great concern.

"The hive leadership is safe, but we need reinforcements immediately."

"My messenger is sending for a sizable group now. They'll be here in minutes."

Sting sighed. "Good. Some of my troops are giving their lives now in the landing grounds to protect their queen. As soon as reinforcements arrive, everybee left from my division should be in sanctuary. Have you set up camp?"

"Yes, I'll have them brought to safety right away."

The two drones continued talking. They gave updates on the practical things of organization, patrols, and sustenance. They shared everything they had learned about their enemies, and Sting's expression hardened with determination as he learned about where Buzzz was stationed.

"So at this very moment, you have troops storming their headquarters?"

"I do."

"I will go there and oversee that. I want you to replenish all the bases we need covered and manage the battle outside." Without hesitation, Sting heaved himself off his blade of grass and started for the rosebush quickly and discreetly. Courage looked on with concern, but he knew that Sting had decided and would not be persuaded otherwise.

Within minutes, reinforcements arrived and Courage directed them into the hive. He gasped in horror at the sheer number of bodies he could see from the chute entrance, yellowjackets and honeybees. They had seemingly been piled to create a barrier to protect the back half of the hive. After giving his directions to various leaders in his army, Courage felt a strong guidance that he couldn't shake to go after Sting. So, he took off. Courage's troops followed the sound of commotion and found the last of Sting's troops, clearly failing in battle against the strength of Buzzz's newcomers.

With a battle cry, the reinforcements went fiercely into the mass. Thereon, hemolymph spilled left and right as bees fell. War was not pretty. It was full of pain, destruction, and loss. But with their renewed strength, Hive Honey Quest was pushing the foreign bees further and further out. Over the next hour, they began to take back control of their hive.

The weakened troops Sting had overseen were able to make their way to the base, and were tended to. Many of Courage's troops and Soldiers who had been waiting eagerly to help went to strengthen the hive base. One significant group had been spotted by a large group of yellowjackets. The clash was impossible to explain with words. Yellowjackets were an extremely dangerous opponent, and many honey bees were losing their lives. Stinger covers were quite possibly the only reason the bees weren't all immediately killed.

This sort of chaos continued for quite some time, and hope was running thin for Hive Honey Quest as their numbers decreased at an alarming rate. Many Soldiers were also losing their lives, and things were not looking agreeable for their victory. Still, they fought, and they fought hard.

Meanwhile, Sting had set out to the rosebush. When he arrived, war had begun there as well. Many yellowjackets and honey bees under Buzzz's rule fought viciously against Hive Honey Quest. Sting had taken a discreet route in, having been aware of the layout from Buzzz's use of this bush in the past. He had but one goal. He was going to confront Buzzz, and if possible, he was going to kill him. The old King pushed on with iron determination until he reached the very room Buzzz used as his headquarters.

For what felt like ages, Sting sat in wait. There were too many bees and yellowjackets going in and out of Buzzz's office to strike just yet. As he watched his father, his blood began to boil.

Buzzz was pacing across the floor, clearly agitated. He shouted orders to every bee who entered his office with great intensity and decisiveness. "I'm going to have to fight, if none of you can do your job properly," he added as one bee left briskly. The old drone had not aged a bit since Sting had last seen him, which was many months ago. He was strong, and as fluid in his gait as ever. His face emanated with a strange and powerful expression that gave Sting a chill down his spine.

It's time for Buzzz to fall. Sting took a breath to shake his nerves and calm his temper. Buzzz was his father, and had mentored him most of his young adult life. And now, all he cared about was regaining power. Sting had to be strong. Then, there was a lull, and the right moment presented itself. With an explosive force, Sting erupted into Buzzz's office, weapons in hand.

He launched himself at his father without hesitation, giving him a sizable scratch on his thorax using a rose thorn. Then, he darted to the side to avoid a counter-attack. Buzzz roared, seemingly caught off guard, but he recovered quickly as ever. The old drone's eyes burned with sick fury.

"Son! Long time no see!" He launched himself back at Sting to leave his own mark on his abdomen. Sting was knocked back, and shrieked in pain.

There was no time for extensive dialogue. It was clear that the only objective each drone had was to kill the other. Sting knew that those protecting Buzzz's office would be joining them soon, and they had not a moment to waste.

The two drones passed each other several times, inflicting considerable wounds. But of the two, Sting was looking worse. During a final pass, Buzzz turned unexpectedly and pierced Sting with a deadly blow to the abdomen using a fresh rose thorn. Sting shrieked and fell to the floor, grasping his wound. Hemolymph trickled from the gash without ceasing and he quickly grew weak. *This is it. I can't defeat him.*

Just then, Hissgaar and other yellowjackets entered the room. Their tall and terrible leader hovered over Sting, a menacing smile of pleasure on his face. He gestured for one of his workers to sting the old king, and he had not a shred of effort left to react or resist. Sting laid there, his body twitching from the strong venom, and the life continued to drain from his body.

Just then, Courage made it through the messy battle to Buzzz's office. He witnessed the final sting, and with a surge more powerful than he could understand or explain, he attacked the yellowjackets. Three were killed from his initial blow, and he didn't stop there. With lightning speed, he lashed at Hissgaar and Buzzz at the same time. The two leaders could hardly see their opponent, but were fierce nonetheless in their defense. Despite that, Courage could not seem to be injured. He fought valiantly against his extremely powerful foes without pause.

JOY LOOKED OVER THE scene, despair in her eyes. The forest had broken into full-on war and Hive Honey Quest was losing. The yellowjackets seemed unstoppable. Her knowledge of them agreed that if this went on any longer, Hive Honey Quest would be no more. Buzzz would win. *He didn't take any chances this time...*

Joy took shelter behind a thickly-vegetated branch to catch her breath. Powerful emotions welled in her chest. *This can't be it, can it? No! This can't be it!" The* With all of the desperation she could muster, she dropped to her knees and shouted out to Lighthive. Her voice carried with such volume that she knew she wouldn't stay hidden from her foes, but she did so nonetheless. "Lighthive, help us! Give us grace on wings!" She heard the deafening buzz of those terrible, vibrant enemies quickly closing in around her crouched body."We can't do this alone. We need YOU!" Tears stained her cheeks as she braced herself for the imminent impact.

Just then, a great fluttering caused a disturbance in the air. Wind swept her foes away from her just before they attacked, and a great sound came from the sky. *Vhooooomm, Vhhhhooooom!* Joy was afraid to open her eyes, but she began to hear the terrible screech of yellowjacket voices being carried away amidst the powerful sound of wings. Finally, she squinted to take in the scene. Much to her amazement, a huge siege of grey and white birds swarmed, creating almost a tornado. Left and right, the birds swiped yellowjackets out of the skies and took them into their beaks.

Joy was wide-eyed now, staring in awe and wonder. *These are Eastern Kingbirds.* They were known to feed on insects, but they didn't really swarm. Joy knew that she was observing nothing short of a miracle. Almost as quickly as the surge came, the birds were lifted from the forest and dissipated into the sky. The loud winds settled, and were followed by an eerie peace.

Slowly, honey bees emerged from their hiding places, blinking in wonder. The birds had taken every remaining yellowjacket, and had left every Hive Honey Quest and Soldier bee untouched. They were frozen in awe and shock. After a few moments, Joy called out with rejoicing. "Lighthive had answered my prayer. Lighthive has saved us today!"

Eventually, the shock wore off and loud cheering erupted from the armies. They shouted out thanks and praises, completely given away to their relief and awe. After several moments like this, the remaining troops slipped off to join the other efforts. Some went to strengthen the hive, and others went to reinforce the attack on the rosebush.

Joy flew toward the rosebush where she believed her brother was. Her heartbeat was so loud as she still swam in the wonder of what just happened. She had witnessed an unexplainable miracle. Lighthive had saved her. Lighthive had saved them. Her faith was on fire. *It's time to finish this.*

Chapter 17: Culmination

Many minutes had passed, and still, Courage functioned from a supernatural strength. Blow after blow continued without pause. His opponents were starting to slow down, a wild fear setting in their eyes.

"What izzz thiszz? Thizzz drone izzz pozzzessed!" Hissgaar shouted between attacks.

Buzzz struggled to say a word as he sluggishly dodged a twentieth attack. His breath seemed to catch in his chest and his body was shaking, deprived of air. Suddenly, Courage stopped. He wasn't phased, and didn't need to recover. His expression was oddly peaceful and radiant. Hissgaar and Buzzz collapsed on the ground, gasping.

Quietly, Courage spoke. "There is a shadow in you." He looked directly at Buzzz, who stared back in fear. "You have given yourself away to the darkness." Courage paced in front of the two leaders.

"Please! Have mercy." Buzzz was begging now, genuinely shaken by this drone. "Who are you?"

"I am Courageous River." The drone replied steadily. "The darkness will always lose against the Light."

"Are you going to kill me?" Buzzz asked shakily. Death seemed to scare him more than anything else.

Courage ignored the question, turning his attention to Hissgaar. "You should know that your entire ranks have been ravaged. Not one remains but you."

The yellowjacket stuttered in disbelief, but could tell that Courage was being truthful. After a few moments, the large drone's eyes filled with great fury as he turned on Buzzz, who still trembled like a child. "You willzz payyyy!" In Buzzz's compromised state, Hissgaar's attack was quickly successful. The yellowjacket drone dealt a killing blow, and Buzzz was dying.

Courage came to himself a bit, and rushed to Sting's side. The drone was still alive, but the venom had worked its way through most of his body by now. The old king fixed his eyes on Courage searchingly.

"It's over. Buzzz is through, and the hive still lives." Courage buzzed, his eyes filling with tears. "You have done well." He held the drone as his expression grew peaceful and warm at those beautiful words..The old king drew his last breath in his grip, and Courage wept.

Buzzz lay dying, and Hissgaar collapsed in exhaustion beside him. Buzzz squirmed uncomfortably as he passed, trembling. "No, no!" His final cry was so desperate and afraid, and then he was gone.

Courage slowly rose to his feet. He turned to look at Hissgaar. The yellowjacket drone dipped his head to him in respect with what little effort he had. "You win." His grumbling voice echoed.

Courage left him, and turned to leave the rosebush. His body began to ache, and he almost collapsed from the shock of his pain. Joy was suddenly right there to catch him. Her eyes sparkling with wonder.

"Brother, your face is glowing!" She helped her limping brother to the rosebush entrance, and he didn't utter a word. She buzzed, "What happened? I see that Buzzz is dead." Courage couldn't seem to speak, and she was patient.

A few minutes later, Courage and Joy met with a large group of bees at the main rosebush entrance. They all looked battle-torn, but full of awe. They had all witnessed the miraculous nature of this battle. They were doomed to lose, but Lighthive helped them. They looked to Courage expectantly.

By now, the drone could speak. "Lighthive has won us this battle. Buzzz is no more. We are free."

The crowd exploded with overwhelming joy for several minutes. When at last they settled, they all made their way back to the hive without another word, Courage and Joy trailing behind at a pace they could keep.

Over the next hours, small groups of bees slowly regrouped back to the hive. A messenger sent for hive leadership in the throne room, and Courage was the only general left to report to them. The hive members were battered and exhausted, and the nurses and doctors were busy tending to them.

Queen Amber came forward to Courage, her expression curious, somber, and proud. "Tell me Courage, what do I need to know?"

Courage collected himself. "Your Highness, HIve Honey Quest is free from danger or threat and will remain so for some time. Lighthive has given us victory."

Joy was at Courage's side, and he gestured for her to describe the miraculous events of the battle that she had witnessed. Queen Amber and King Justice's eyes were alight with interest. After she concluded her tale, Courage continued.

"Many many bees have been lost, including our king of late, Sting. He gave up his life in a valiant effort to win this war. I was able to finish the job and give him peace in his final moments." Courage dipped his head.

Queen Amber nodded. "Good. As you can tell, we have defeated those who infiltrated the hive too. We've won. Our queen of late, Royal, and her nurse bee Nectar have just passed though." She was somber. "Thank you for your service, and your information. Please see that the Hive of Soldiers is thanked and sent home well fed. Then, please arrange for the fixing of this desecrated home of ours so we can pick ourselves up again."

Courage bowed in respect. "Queen Amber, Hive Honey Quest will enter a golden era, and you will be at its head. May you and King Justice find your strength and wisdom in Lighthive."

Queen Amber smiled. "And we shall." Turning to Joy, she smiled again. "Your insight and contribution in this war was absolutely necessary for our victory. You will be rewarded, and can take a leadership role here if you are ready."

Joy's eyes lit up. "Me? Oh, I'd be honored! I'll help however I can!"

"Start by helping Courge with those tasks."

Joy and Courage went on to organize everything needed. The Hive of Soldiers were asked to have their fill of honey before the trip home. There was a brief ceremony to thank them all, in which many tears were shed for the losses of both Hive Honey Quest and the Hive of Soldiers. The wounded were being tended to and the dead were being cleared from the hive for several hours.

In a moment of rest, Joy rested her head on her brother's shoulder as they sat. "It's over. It's all over." The relief in her voice was apparent.

"Peace and prosperity lay ahead." Courage smiled weakly, his body racked with pain and weakness.

"Are you okay brother?"

"I am. And I have a feeling that soon it will be my time to leave Hive Honey Quest."

Joy turned her face to him with sad eyes. She tilted her head. "Will you finally be off to join your lovely young queen?"

Courage smiled with warmth. "Yes, I think I will." He looked at his sister. "But know, I will always be with you sister. And I'll visit whenever I can."

Joy was smiling, but her face portrayed many emotions. Sadness, fear, heartbrokenness. On top of that, a deep curiosity. "There is something about you that I don't know, isn't there?"

Courage paused, a bit taken off-guard and unsure of how to respond.

Joy peered at him. "There is not another like you in existence, I think. You are remarkably in sync with the Light, like one well beyond your months. I don't think you've ever made a wrong decision in your life." Courage opened his mouth to respond, but Joy continued. "And, you carry an air of mystery. I feel as though you are many bees in one, or guarding many secrets. I can't properly explain it, but it's different. I don't need you to tell me, Courage." Joy gestured for Courage to relax and stay silent. "You, brother, are remarkable. You are unearthly. And I feel incredibly lucky to have had you as a dear friend. You have no idea how much you've impacted me."

Joy stared at Courage meaningfully. Her eyes portrayed a great restraint over desperate curiosity. "I only hope to understand, one day. Whenever it is fit for me to know." She looked at Courage again with warmth, and pulled him in for a sisterly hug. When she pulled away, Courage spoke.

"Whatever you see in me, thank the Light." It seemed like all he could bear to say. He longed for Joy to know about his secret life, but he just never felt free to share. There was something so sacred about it, and he felt that it was not meant to be known until the end of life. Still, he looked forward to the day that all would be known and understood. One day, he and his dear sister could dwell together in that golden-lit forest. Looking at Joy, he buzzed. "Dear sister, you've been a great blessing to me as well. You exude passion, optimism, and a mental clarity. When I go, I will spend a lot of time missing you. And I will go in peace knowing that you will help this hive forth into an era of priceless peace and blessing."

The two stood together in silence for a few minutes, the hive bustling about them. Like this they remained until they parted to their cells for much needed rest.

Chapter 18: Of Other Hives

Amethyst stared blankly at the wall, in a stupor of sorts. She simply could not believe her ears. Her King and many of her offspring had been killed, and there was nothing left for her. She knew that Hissgaar and whatever remained of his kin would be after her soon if she didn't leave.

The queen bee had stayed in Buzzz's home base during the battle. Messengers had come once a day to update her on the situation, and she had spent her time laying more eggs and tending to her newly emerging young. At this time, she had close to a thousand new children. But being that she was now alone, she couldn't shake the paralysis she felt.

Amethyst had placed all of her value in Buzzz. She held onto the highest highs and buckled under his lowest lows. She simply didn't know how to exist without him. Her grief was terrible, and profoundly confusing. She also felt a powerful relief, but was currently not capable of putting voice to that part of her emotions. Subconsciously, the queen also felt safe for the first time in a long time. Safe, but completely lost. She knew not what lay ahead.

She spent most of the day like this, swimming in the confusion of her subconscious thoughts and doing nothing else. But Hissgaar would be coming soon, and the weight of that knowledge nagged her with increasing force.

One of Amethyst's daughters entered the room meekly. She looked at her mother's lost expression, and sat beside her. After a few minutes and a gentle touch on the arm, she buzzed. "What's next?"

Amethyst's mouth opened, then closed. After several moments, she buzzed quietly in response. "I have no idea. I... have nothing."

The worker moved closer to her mother with caution. "I'm here for you." The queen turned her empty gaze to her daughter, the tiniest spark of recognition in her eyes, and her daughter continued speaking. "You are our queen. All we need is you, and we can make it through this."

"I am nothing without him."

"No, you are everything this hive needs right now. And if you can somehow lead us through this, then one day we can truly thrive for the first time." The she-bee was silent for a few minutes, as her queen received her words. Then, she pressed on. "Mother, let's look for a suitable place and build our own home. I'm sure we can do better than this old trunk."

Amethyst looked around, for once observing the conditions with new eyes. Her gaze drifted to her isolated cell in the far corner. Her stone cold eyes softened and began welling with huge tears as she started to realize how she'd been living. She felt ashamed. How had she found herself in this situation? She'd had such high hopes for life. For love. She'd been innocent and naive, optimistic and hopeful.

The queen let the tears flow as she truly felt the shock and pain of her position. It hurt to feel, but it was better than being numb. She turned to cry on her daughter's shoulder for a long time. "I am a failure..."

"No!" The she-bee cried. "No. We aren't finished. There is light ahead."

After crying for a while, Amethyst raised her chin. Her face was set with determination and a new fire. "It is time to evacuate. Now. I won't have my children suffer for my inaction." Her daughter nodded curtly and the two rose.

"What about the eggs?" The worker asked feebly.

The queen sighed with regret. "Either some of us will escape, or none of us will. We have to leave them." She wiped her tears away with resolve, casting one last longing look at the nursery comb. Before turning away in defeat, her face lit up as an idea came to her. The queen wordlessly proceeded to pack each egg cell with a fresh supply of food, and then as her daughter watched, she took pieces of bark from around the room and tried her best to conceal the nursery comb. It took some time but by the end of this, they were quite hidden behind the bark and hardly noticeable. "Perhaps we can check back for them in a few days. With caution, of course."

The two she-bees continued on, and queen Amethyst addressed her young. She decided she would search in the west, past the boundary of Hive Honey Quest's farm and pollination grounds. And maybe, just maybe, she'd be able to network with them or other branch-off hives. She wondered how her sisters were doing - the other queens from the games. *Better than I am, I hope.*

As Amethyst and her daughter approached the entrance to the hive, there was a sound. The two bees jumped, immediately prepared to face danger. But from the outside, a gentle voice called.

"Is there anyone in there?" The voice was that of a drone.

Amethyst recognized it, but it was not a voice that would strike fear into her heart. *Who is that?* Creeping cautiously toward the light, she offered a response. "Yes, we are here. Who are you?" As her eyes adjusted, she saw a small group of Hive Honey Quest bees before her. The group seemed to be led by the drone, who's name she couldn't quite remember. She had noticed him during the queen games, but had never gotten his name.

"We've come looking for survivors. The hive has won, thank Lighthive! But one of the enemies mentioned something about a stolen queen, trying to taunt us. We decided to track this queen down, and here we are!" The drone's gentle expression swelled with accomplishment.

"Oh!" Amethyst fixed her hesitant eyes on the drone, suddenly taken by his overall countenance. He exuded such... such... *humility, yet charisma... masculinity but gentleness!* She tried to slow her thoughts. *He's just a drone. I can't entertain a connection right now. I have other priorities.* Straightening, she blinked and adjusted her stance. "Well, we are very grateful for your concern! My offspring and I are safe, and we are going to establish our own hive far away from this awful place." She smiled.

The drone shifted. "There's no pressure, but our crew would be happy to join you."

The queen paused. "As in, to help build a new hive?"

"Yes." The drone's eyes sparkled with cautious excitement.

Amethyst thought for a moment. How could she trust this group of bees? There weren't too many to keep in check if need be, but her heart wanted to reject help. How could she trust her own judgment again? As the queen contemplated, she regarded a sudden and overpowering feeling deep within. Peace. The more she considered the thought, the more peace she felt. There was no more fear, uncertainty, or dissent. This was a feeling Amethyst hadn't felt before, and she knew she could trust it, if not herself.

"We would love to have you." The small band of Hive Honey Quest bees cheered with excitement at this response, and the leading drone smiled as they celebrated. Amethyst looked at him again, keeping a rein on the connection she felt with him. "And you, sir, what's your name?"

"I'm Theo. Amethyst, right?" His countenance took on a sweet sort of awkwardness, indicating that perhaps he wasn't always the smoothest talker. He dipped his head, and his eyes betrayed a gleam of well restrained mutual regard for the young queen. For a moment, the two looked into the other's eyes, and a spark was felt.

"Yes, I'm Amethyst." The queen smiled and dipped her head before breaking contact to delegate tasks to her young. The arrivals pitched in however they could to help in the preparations.

When they were ready, Queen Amethyst, her offspring, Theo, and the newcomers were off to seek out their new home. That growing sense of peace filled Amethyst's heart the further she departed from the dark place they'd lived. She took a deep breath, taking in the scent of fresh nectar around her, and was enlivened. There was new hope and purpose, and even the possibility of real love in her future. And while the path ahead was full of trials and uncertainty, Amethyst shook her wings and allowed herself to feel free again. *May I never be a slave again.*

AFTER BUZZZ'S DEATH, Hissgaar and his meager troop of nestmates made their way back home with great haste. They did in fact stop at Buzzz's old home, determined to destroy anything or anybee that remained there. They found nothing. With great frustration, Hissgaar sped towards his home with his troop, hoping to regroup with those who stayed at the nest.

The truth was, the colony's queen had died around two weeks before the battle. She had fallen sick a month before her death and had stopped laying eggs. In their stubbornness, they hadn't made the immediate choice to raise new queens out of her last brood, and they remained overly optimistic that she'd recover. But despite efforts to save her, she continued to decline in spite of her youth. As her last eggs began to hatch, she still hadn't laid more. The yellowjackets now had no hope of remaining a functioning colony without a producing queen.

You may remember how a queen bee was given to Hissgaar to produce honey bees for him and the nest. The timid queen, Blossom, had undergone great turmoil for a few weeks before the war began. Her first batch of young were lost. But then, the war began. The nest was left largely unguarded, as most of the yellowjackets joined the fight. In their absence, Blossom had produced a thousand more bees each day. As they emerged from the comb, she and her offspring quickly outnumbered her foes, and she led them in a great rebellion.

In a matter of two days, Blossom had secured the nest. The once fearful and hesitant queen had blossomed into her strength, since she knew she had no other choice. Her leadership was aflame with a desire to live and preserve the lives of her offspring. Very quickly, she had ordered the building of a hive nearby and was transferring newly hatched bees to that place as they came.

And so, Hissgaar could never have expected what he was entering into when he arrived home. He and his meager company exploded into hisses and shrieks as they realized they had nothing left here. Bodies of their dead nestmates piled near the entrance, and shreds of paper hung left and right. The place was tattered, and seemingly abandoned. Their firefly servants had been set free, and the honey bees were nowhere in sight. The empty nursery comb stood stark against the nest's materials.

Yellowjackets were tough, but some things could easily spook them. The desecration of their home was enough to send them reeling into superstitious fear. What could have caused this? How could they have possibly fallen this far? What great force was against them?

Before long, they exited in an odd and feverish frenzy. The last remaining creatures scattered and flew, each toward some kind of certain death. Water, a clearing where birds hunted, a hot stone under the burning sun. And with that, the yellowjackets from this nest were no more.

Neither Blossom nor Amethyst's brood were lost, and all larvae who survived eventually transformed into bees. These bees were able to join their mother's new hives in the wild, and the two hives stayed connected to help one another survive. And so, every dark force that had plotted against Hive Honey Quest was completely destroyed and lived no more.

The two new wild hives would have a difficult path ahead, but each would also have some special force on their side. They would grow into modest but thriving hives, able to sustain themselves without HoneyBandit intervention for generations.

Meanwhile, the Hive of Soldiers were strong and prominent as ever. Their roots ran deep, and their devotion to Lighthive protected them. They had losses in this great war, but recovered well as always. They continued to instill character and bravery into each new generation of soldiers. Their alliance with Hive Honey Quest would continue amicably for generations to come, though with a welcome uneventful nature.

And so, all hives around Hive Honey Quest would thrive and benefit from its coming years of peace. The sweet nectar of flowers would flow and disease would be minimal. Natural predators would seem to avoid the general area for several seasons. A supernatural protection would cover the land.

Chapter 19: Remembrance

Allow me to take you back to Hive Honey Quest and the aftermath of this final and deciding war.

As after any war, there was much to repair. Several wounded bees were able to recover while some were lost. The hive needed much reconstruction and cleaning after its infiltration, and thousands of bees tended to that work. Other bees could resume the functions of day to day life, from pollination and honey making to beedances and rest at night.

Unlike after the War of the Ghost, there was a great and undeniable sense of light within the hive. War was ugly and destructive, but their wonder and awe for the miraculous provision within this war gave them a hunger for truth. Many began seeking Lighthive in a very earnest and personal way. Courage stayed to help mentor seeking bees for a few weeks after the battle, and he saw a great awakening within them.

Among those who made great changes was Theo. The guarded, self-seeking drone had truly cracked open. Over the last months, Courage had the pleasure of being there for him through that process. He got to see the old drone do what many couldn't. Chains within his heart were broken, even though he had repeatedly chosen differently in the past. His heart softened and for the first time, he put others above himself. Theo had begun to serve the hive in incredible ways, and had also fought valiantly and selflessly during the final battle.

Many bees struggled to trust him and accept this new behavior, but Theo pressed on and continued without batting an eye. He no longer needed others to see him, and he no longer thirsted for power and recognition. Soon enough he began to win back the trust of many. Such a miraculous transformation Courage had never witnessed before. It gave him great joy, and strengthened his desire to be home once again where all was right.

Theo's story was complicated, but it was never too late for him to be free. And free indeed he was. Courage remembered his last session with the drone.

"I was so ashamed... of all I did. But then, the Light stopped me in my path. I heard from within, 'You have done many wrongs. You have stepped away from that life, and you are forgiven. Take hold of this new day, and dwell not on the insufficiency of your past. It's not about you anymore.'" The drone's eyes shone. "Some bees might be offended by that, but for me, it felt like a huge weight was lifted. It's not about me anymore. I could be rid of myself... my old self. I could take on a new identity and live for something better." Theo had grasped Courage's hand, tears glistening in his eyes. "I am forever changed."

Courage had noted the beauty of the drone's countenance. From stubborn, cold, and self-seeking as he was, to humble, confident, and outwardly focused. He was abandoned - completely free from his obsession with image and recognition. No other bee or title or honor defined him anymore. He was made totally new, and surely had a bright future ahead. It was a bittersweet farewell when Theo decided to seek out Queen Amethyst. The drone had felt that he was called there, and without hesitation had heeded that call. Courage blessed the journey, and hoped that Theo's life could be full of goodness and happiness.

Courage and Joy both held positions of leadership in the hive system. Queen Amber and King Justice ran things very well, and were really settling into their new roles. The King was a fiery drone with a taste for humor and adventure. His influence in the hive encouraged all kinds of passion and excitement. Queen Amber was steady and focused. Her stability centered the hive and nurtured it into a place of safety and harmony. Together, the two led with balance and were highly respected by the hive.

Sugar, Amber's nurse bee, also grew proficient into her role. She was a unique combination of spiritual and realist. She was often quite matter-of-fact, and Amber came to appreciate her direct way of being. Sugar was never afraid to say exactly what needed to be said, and her input proved priceless.

With a passion for the Honeycrystal and all things Lighthive, Sugar helped foster new faith in the hive. She led many trips to the crystal and was always there for bees who had questions. Despite her direct nature, she spoke with particular grace and understanding toward anyone who came to her for advice. She bore herself with humility, knowing that the most important thing was not to be their everything, but to point them toward the source.

It was much because of Sugar that the hive would not become overly religious and ritualistic. Instead, she had a knack for helping others foster their love for the Light within. There was a great unity beneath it all, but also room for each bee to bring something a little different to the table. There was passionate conversation and a place for questioning. In this delicate balance, each bee was growing into who they were meant to be. The result would be an incredibly rare perfection of earthly existence.

So as it was foretold, Hive Honey Quest was headed into a supernatural season of true and lasting peace.

Meanwhile, Royal, Sting, and Nectar were all being honored tonight with a grand ceremony. While their bodies had been removed from the hive weeks ago at their deaths, the hive had been unable to sit in remembrance at that time with all that was going on. So, now was the time to honor the lost cornerstones of Hive Honey Quest. Joy was given the responsibility of much of the planning, and she did a wonderful job.

In the newly cleaned and refreshed landing grounds, there were several long tables with acorn shell chairs. She must have had bees gathering materials for weeks. Strings of vining flowers decorated the walls and tables elegantly. The vines were freshly picked, and their nectar was particularly sweet. The hive slowly gathered at the end of the productive day, ready to reminisce on their old hive leaders' memory.

At the podium, Queen Amber, King Justice, and Sugar stood. Others were going to speak first, since they had known the deceased for much longer. Once the hive had gathered, Queen Amber signaled for silence and the crowd became still. "Thank you all for being here to honor our leaders of late. Please allow Courage to speak on their lives." She stepped aside for the drone.

Courage stood, silent for a moment before he began. "Hive Honey Quest. Our hive has had quite the unfavorable reputation over the years. I've had the privilege of hearing the history from Sting himself. And for those of you who don't know, I will share it.

"Our hive is domestic, tended to by HoneyBandits. And for whatever reason, the hive thrived here. Word spread far and wide about our incredible production of honey and our resilient nature toward the challenges each hive must face. Whether from the beginning or by some odd mutation, our drones became known for longevity. This was both an object of wonder, and of scrutiny. Was it something to be praised or something twisted? Well, it certainly bent the rules of nature, and created an environment for unusual hive dynamics.

"A typical hive is valuable because of its queen. But Hive Honey Quest quickly shifted as prominent and powerful drones came into leadership. Here, it became standard practice to have a King. This King would outlive his queen. And over time, this dynamic shifted the very nature of things. Prominent drones became power hungry, and soon, usurped the absolute leadership of their Queen. This leads me to our story, and our more recent history.

"Queen Lilac and King Buzzz ruled Hive Honey Quest. As Lilac grew in age, the HoneyBandits sent for a new queen. At that time, Buzzz and many of his respected sons held great power in the hive. They enforced strict rules about how each bee lived. No one could have a thought that challenged his total supremacy. Faith was squelched, and anybee who brought it up would be killed. Perfect order and function were expected, with no room for enjoyment or free expression. This was the hive that Queen Royal and her daughters were lowered into. Let us take a moment to remember Love, Peace, Trust, Faith, and Hope. Each daughter had to face this hive, having been taken from a place that honored Lighthive.

"Royal and Sting's union was an arranged one. Sting had studied under his father Buzzz, and the tyrant believed fully that his son was of like mind. She faced joining with a stranger - someone she didn't know and couldn't trust - just days after arriving here. Shortly after this, Royal and her daughters began drumming up a rebellion. With impressive speed, skill, and secrecy, they were able to build an army within that could stand up to Buzzz's tyrannical leadership. By chance it seemed, they were able to connect with the Hive of Soldiers and establish an alliance.

"Royal sensed that her mate was not like his father. With patience and strategy, she worked on him, seeking the amity she felt could be possible with him. And eventually, the King took the first step and broke free from his father's control. King Sting had spent a lifetime of brainwashing, but with a strong heart, was able to break the cycle. His strength is incredible. Together, they secretly built the rebellion, and when the time was right, there was war. The War of the Ghost.

"Though it wasn't easy or even expected, the rebellion won this war. But it was just the beginning of a long journey which lay ahead. The entire hive was accustomed to the way of tyrannical leadership. They were lost! How could they learn to think for themselves again when all there was before was fear? And so, phase two of change came. During this time, many bees were disjointed and troubled. Royal oversaw the delicate and difficult task of strengthening the individuality of each hive member. She gently introduced the option of faith, believing in her heart that it was the way to happiness and purpose. But unlike with prior leadership, she did not force her will upon the members of the hive. She instead fostered growth within them-growth that many chose to nurture.

"As one could expect, many hive members were struggling with the transition after Buzzz's reign. The New Beginning cult formed in the shadows of the hive, and many bees latched onto this familiar feeling of structure and comfort. And so the hive faced a season of alarming inner turmoil. Some bees found healing and growth over time, while others became even more lost than before. The cult group eventually challenged Royal and Sting, but ultimately without success. New Beginning was then dissolved, and rehabilitation again became our focus.

"After a promising season, many more hive members were able to realize their freedom, and explore what that meant for them. Mentorship was available, and many began to grow in faith. We started to see a healthier hive. But waiting in the shadows, the ghost of our past was preparing for his return. Buzzz had been badly injured in the war, but not killed. Ever since his departure, he spent all of his energy building an army to try and take back what he believed to be his.

"Thanks to divine knowledge, we were able to prepare for this. We were not caught off guard. And thanks to Lighthive's protection and undeniable involvement, we have been able to finally earn total freedom from the ghosts of our past. In the very same moment, Royal, Sting, and Nectar were gone.

"Royal led us through this turmoil, and yet never got to taste the total freedom she'd nurtured in us during her lifetime. Still, she set us all up for lives of true success. She dedicated her life to making ours bright. Her wisdom and connection to the Light made it possible for us to be where we are today.

"King Sting worked through some of the most difficult identity struggles and came through better for it. He led with strength, wisdom, and compassion. He and Royal fell deeply in love, and their bond inspired everybee around them. Their unity and strength together was unmatched. His skills in battle and management were perhaps one of the key reasons why we are still here today.

"Nectar was the best nurse bee. She stood by her queen, and they flowed together like a river. Her intrigue, her passion, and her endless knowledge fueled hive leadership and enabled them to lead so much better. She was selfless, competent, and truly unique. Anybee who knew her was privileged.

"And so, we look back with gratitude on our late leaders, and the way they gave all of themselves in order to give *us* the chance of hope. May we never forget or take for granted that priceless gift. May we praise Lighthive forever, the force behind each of these prominent bees and the reason we've been so blessed."

Courage concluded his speech, and the crowd remained in silent vigil for several minutes. Throughout the evening, other small speeches were given and hymns sung. Following this was a reverent prayer to Lighthive and a grand feast to honor and remember all that had come and passed. From this night on, it would be a very long time before anybee forgot how blessed they were.

Chapter 20: Farewell

It was the day after the ceremony for Royal, Sting, and Nectar. Courage sat on his pollen-stuffed cushion with a bittersweet heart. He had been visited by Meadow that night in a dream, and he closed his eyes to revel in the memory.

Her beautiful form flew toward him with eagerness, and tears of joy soaking her face. "It is time! Oh River, you have fulfilled your purpose with such grace!" She took hold of him, and they spun together on the mossy forest floor. Courage let himself laugh with pure joy, his heart yearning to be home for good.

"Meadow, I can't wait to be here all the time once again - to regain any shred of memory I still haven't recovered. I can't imagine I've ever loved you more."

The queen took his face into her hands, their antennae entwined. "My Love, I can't wait."

"How can I come back to you?" Courage buzzed, his face warm.

"Come to the valley beneath the Honeycrystal. Unlike others, you will be able to enter into eternity for the last time. You will say goodbye to the brokenness of this world."

Courage's face fell just slightly. "I will miss my dear sister Joy. I hope that one day, she'll dwell with us in this perfect valley."

"She will." Meadow smiled. "But don't you remember, this valley is just the outskirts of the light."

Courage looked surprised. "Oh? I must have forgotten!"

"No one can see the fullness of the Light and stay alive! I should have known it would stay from your memory. Oh Courage, it is more beautiful than you could ever imagine or describe. And this time, you won't ever have to leave again."

Courage soaked in the wonder and longing he felt. "The Light... I will get to swim in its presence?"

"Yes. And it's more perfect than our love. It can not be captured or explained with any words. But you have glimpsed it in life, and here in this forest. It is perfect and total freedom. There will be no sorrow, no pain, no struggle, and no bondage. Just love, safety, perfection, beauty, and praise. Forevermore."

Courage came back to himself in his cell. After hearing this from Meadow, the world felt even less real and even less like home. He walked out of his door, almost in a dream-like state. He first made his way to the throne room to speak with hive leadership. Courage had prepared them that he'd soon leave, so they wouldn't be shocked.

At the door of the throne room, two guards nodded to let him pass. Queen Amber and King Justice sat together at the center of the room as he entered. He dipped his head in respect, waiting to be addressed.

"Courage, welcome!" Queen Amber buzzed. "What brings you here?"

Courage took a breath, his face portraying what he was about to say. "Queen Amber, it's time for me to go."

She pursed her lips, disappointment in her eyes. "I see. When?"

"Today."

"Will you stay for a goodbye party tonight?"

Courage smiled. "That is very nice of you, but no. I'll be going by sunhigh, and saying my goodbyes this morning."

Amber sighed. "You, Courage, will be greatly missed. Your service to this hive has not only been impactful, but also essential. I want to thank you for all you've done here." The Queen stood from her throne and bowed deeply before him with great respect and gratitude. Justice dipped his head with approval toward the older drone.

"Where are you off to, Courage? Perhaps our hives can be in communication in the future." King Justice asked.

Courage looked at him, a glimmer of mystery in his eyes. "I'll be going a great distance, but I won't be too far. I'm sure we can connect again. I'll reach out to you if and when that time comes."

The King was satisfied, and he and his Queen said their goodbyes. Courage left the throne room with a skip in his step. *One step closer to eternity...* He spent the morning speaking briefly with various passerbees who he'd mentored. Each hive member had come to mean so much to him. He felt great peace now that in his absence, prosperity could continue for a very long time. They had the tools now to truly thrive.

The sun climbed higher, and Courage was ready to leave. The last bee he would say farewell to would be his dear sister Joy. She knew he was leaving, and waited for him at the hive entrance. When he came into her view, she looked at him with warmth and sadness before giving him a giant hug. Tears fell onto Courage's furry coat as she gripped him.

"Brother, I love you so much! I will miss you dearly."

"And I you!" Courage held on tight, water collecting in his eyes too. When they pulled apart, they gazed at each other with fondness. "Joy, you are a marvel. I know you will take care of this hive and its inhabitants in my stead."

"I will do my very best."

"And love the Light, sister. It will be your strength and your safe place."

Joy smiled. "Yes, brother. I do, and I will."

Courage gave her one more hug, and waved back at her once again before taking off into the sunlight. It was a perfect day. The breeze was gentle and refreshing, and the world was bathed in a pleasant glow. Courage closed his eyes, taking a deep breath in and out. He changed his direction to head toward the valley at the foot of the Honeycrystal's mountain. *Homeward bound.*

SUGAR SAT ALONE IN the quiet. She was in the room that Nectar had most often taught her in. She thought about her dear mentor with warmth and fondness. *I will always keep missing her, I think.* Closing her eyes, she practiced calming her mind and focusing on the peace she had within. Just like Nectar had taught her, she redirected her mind back to the light whenever it strayed. Soon, her thoughts were settled in a place of comfort and safety rather than wandering. Like this, she sat for several minutes.

Doing this truly gave her mind rest. It restored her, and gave her a chance to hear from the Light. Most times, she didn't need to hear anything. But this time, her spirit perked up to the feeling of the following words.

"A time of unexplainable peace comes. Steward your gifts with grace and wisdom. Never forget that from which they came. Revel in the reward for your faith, and give thanks daily."

Sugar quietly jotted down the words that flowed through her.

"The Light is your protector and your source. Come to know it. Let it overflow from your being into the lives of everybee around you. You have been given much, so give freely to others."

After a few moments in silence, Sugar stirred and stretched. She looked down at her birch bark paper and read those words again, letting them sink in. Her heart was ripe with joy and hope for the future, and the peace she felt was astounding. In that moment, she truly believed that nothing could shake her. Nothing else mattered like these truths did. She held the paper close to her chest, and whispered. "Thank you."

~THE END~

Also by Amarah Parks

Hive Honey Quest
Hope
Faith
Courage

Watch for more at https://www.instagram.com/amarahparks/.

About the Author

Amarah enjoys a quiet life in Minnesota with her amazing husband, adorable two year old son, and precious baby girl. In addition to writing, she enjoys creating and releasing music as well as raising competetive show rabbits.

Read more at https://www.instagram.com/amarahparks/.

www.ingramcontent.com/pod-product-compliance
Lightning Source LLC
Chambersburg PA
CBHW022143150726
47992CB00002B/738